# Midnight Inferno

## by

### A. M. Keen

Published under license from Andrews UK

# The Missing

"Get down!"

"What? What is it?"

Brent peered through the shrubbery as a small, amber light appeared in the darkness. "It looks like a lamp, or torch, or something?" He scoured the gloom as distant footfalls broke debris atop the woodland floor.

Jay shuffled beside him. "You see anyone?" His voice trembled with every word.

A shiver passed along Brent's spine. The pungent aroma of damp bracken filled the air. The cool breeze of a late spring swirled within the greenery. The canopy above swayed and rattled with each gust. Those footfalls drew closer. A bird cawed in the distance, its call echoing the length and breadth of the woodland they explored.

He turned back to Jay. "Just stay the hell down." The amber glow of a lantern illuminated the leaves. "Shit!" Brent contained his fear no longer. A man, huge in stature, held the historic light source at arm's length. A long, wiry beard protruded from his jaw. Greasy, shoulder-length hair swept across his face. The giant's hand emerged, pushing the wayward strands back. Brent trembled as the man stopped, scouring the area, shining the lamp in every direction.

"Who's out here?" the giant shouted. His voice bellowed with malice. Brent gasped, holding his breath. The man squinted, one eye larger than the other. "I heard you!"

*'Go away! Just go away!'* Brent's eyes closed. An image of both he and Jay appeared within his mind. Captured by this behemoth, they lay across his gargantuan shoulders, carried to the dilapidated farm from whence he came. There, they would be tortured and maimed, hidden from the rest of the world and their parents, forever. Why the hell hadn't he just stayed home and done his homework?

The man smiled. "It's not safe out here. Strange things happen in these woods, things you can never imagine." The woodland swayed about them, brought to life by the rushing winds.

Through the leaves, the shrubbery and the beat of his own heart, a snap intruded Brent's fear.

The man wiped a dirty hand across an even dirtier shirt. Even through the beard, an expression of concern appeared. A light flashed.

"You need to leave with me, now!"

White flashes illuminated the trees. Brent peered from his hiding place to see electricity jump between the surrounding branches and trunks. The man, unsettled, looked about the woodland. His chest heaved with every breath.

"I'm warning you!"

The voltage increased and snapped throughout the area. Forked lightning jolted overhead. Wind powered throughout the trees.

Brent turned over his shoulder. "We gotta run!"

"What?" Jay cried, his voice no more than a whisper behind the roaring elements.

"Now!"

Brent launched from the ground, drawing the man's attention. "Hey? Hey!"

Brent ignored the voice, turned his back and bounded through the trees. Jay followed.

"No!" the man bellowed. Lightning streamed across the sky. "No!"

Brent peered over his shoulder. *'Keep running! Keep running!'* Electricity thrashed about them. Earth exploded, struck by the element as it crashed down in to the ground. Tree bark blew from the trunks, torn by forks that lashed between them. A flash, temporary blinding, struck the ground in Brent's path, destroying the terrain and searing soil in to the air. He tumbled sideways, placing a hand down to keep balance.

"Brent!"

Brent turned. Jay, engulfed by lightning, reached out to him. His expression twisted with fear. "Help me!" he screamed. Forks lashed from each direction, clasping his limbs. "God, help me!"

The ground rumbled. Jay lofted upward. Lightning snapped about his body, binding him in white light.

Brent dropped, falling to the ground face first. Lightning coiled at his ankle. He turned, clawing at the vegetation. Light flashed and wrapped about his wrists. The burning, stinging sensation struck in an instant. Brent screamed, fighting against the restraints. His skin smouldered within its grasp. Liquid oozed from its hold, dropping to the earth in crimson streams. Lightning thrashed from each direction, grasping and lifting him in to the air. Jay wailed in the distance. The bearded man stood, inverted in Brent's eye-line, watching, only watching. Light flashed again. He swayed, upside down, throttled by his binding. Hair danced across his face.

The ground, as unforgiving as it was, knocked the wind from his body. Brent heaved on impact and rolled a distance across the damp terrain. He dare not open his eyes. Light burned pink beyond the eyelids he screwed shut. A hand grasped his shoulder.

"God, Brent, oh shit! Look!"

Brent opened his eyes. White light engulfed the woodland, hiding every tree behind its beauty. From its aura, five silhouettes emerged, slim, dark, almost religious with a graceful approach. Walking toward them, palms outward, they glided to the fallen boys, still mere shadows against a burning light.

# 1

A solitary pair of headlights passed in the other lane, the only vehicle he'd seen in half an hour or so. Darkness engulfed the horizon as the journey continued, but the last road sign explained his destination not much further on. The cell phone lighted from its holder on the dash.

"Agent Cane. How are you?"

Cane recognised the voice as his senior, Division Leader Weston. "Almost there, sir."

"Good, good. Did you get the dossier?"

Cane looked to the passenger seat where a brown envelope lay. "Yes sir. I've read the briefing, but will give it my utmost attention when I arrive."

"Make sure you do, Agent. This may be the most important assignment anyone has undertaken within this division."

"Of course, sir." Lights appeared beside the road that looked like a bar, or motel, or something.

"The tracking system is expecting some kind of contact within the next few days, make sure you're there."

"Does Intel know where, exactly?"

"Negative, only that it's narrowed to that one town and its surrounding area."

Cane shook his head. "Okay, sir. Leave it with me. As soon as I find anything I'll report back."

"Good luck, Cane."

"Thank you."

Cane ended the call and sighed. A white sign appeared across the road, welcoming him to Millers Fall in elegant lettering. He missed the population.

The lights did indeed belong to a motel. Cane pulled in to the lot, now aware of how tired he'd become.

The car shimmered to a standstill, parked outside the neon light reading 'Reception' in a panel window. The other sign illuminated red through the darkness, informing of vacancies to be had this evening.

The reception area appeared cosy. Varnished floorboards, panelled walls, some kind of indoor tree stood vibrant in the corner. The blinds about him had been closed, but not quite. *King of Queens* played out on the TV, watched by a clerk behind the desk across the room.

"Evening." The clerk sat upright in the chair. Behind him a row of keys mounted the wall, and a door to god-knows-where stood ajar.

"Hi. I'm looking for a room this evening."

The clerk smiled. "You came to the right place, my friend." He appeared no more than thirty years old. A weak attempt at facial hair curled in patches from his upper lip and chin. "We got standard or luxury available this evening?"

"What's the difference?"

"With standard you have everything you come to expect from a motel, TV, bathroom, et cetera, but with luxury your bath is bigger, queen-sized double, mini bar and access to pay per view, all included."

"How much?"

"Standard is fifty bucks a night, luxury ninety five."

"Wow. That's actually pretty cheap, if you don't mind me saying?"

The clerk laughed. "It sure is. This whole site has been paid for. We only charge for utilities. We're right on a crossroads that leads to Port Sandown, Portland, and the various other towns out to the west. Cheaper rooms in a busy area equal more business."

"They certainly do. I'll go luxury, please."

"Fantastic." The clerk flipped open a guest book, finding the next available line. "Pop your name and signature in here please."

Agent Cane smiled as he grasped a pen and filled out his details.

"Not taken the leap in to the twenty first century, then?"

"Don't need to. Books are just as good at storing data, at least for this place."

"Do you serve food at all?" he asked, whilst writing his name. The swollen, bubble-like sensation harbouring deep inside had decided it was time to eat.

The clerk grimaced whilst turning to the keys. "Only got snacks in the vending machine and mini bar I'm afraid. But, if you head on in to The Fall on this road, you'll come to Ellie's Diner on the left. My brother owns it." He turned back, handing key number five across.

"The Fall?"

The clerk rolled his eyes. "Yeah, sorry. Millers Fall. Locals call it The Fall for short. If you head up to Ellie's, though, tell them I sent you, you'll get your meal cheaper. We have a business relationship. You know, sending customers to each other? He doesn't close up until ten, so you still got time. You have your photo ID?"

"Sure." Cane opened his wallet, fumbling for the card inside. "It's about the only thing I got, though."

The clerk took the plastic, scouring the photo and name against the register. "That's great, Mister Cane."

"My name is Emmett."

The clerk extended his hand after returning the card. "Ben. Ben Latcham." The two shook hands. "How long you staying for?"

Cane sighed. "In all honesty, I don't know for sure. I'm in to real estate, and I'm scouting some buildings to develop in the area. Like you said, the town has some great advantages. Central location, you know, it's good for both work and family. I hear many good things about Millers Fall so thought I'd head this way and see for myself."

"Well, it's a sleepy little town. If peace and quiet is your thing, then this place is exactly what you're looking for."

Cane nodded. "This is my town for sure. Do I need to pay upfront for any extra days? If I book in for three nights now, can I add more when I know what I'm doing?"

"I can reserve the room for you, if you want to stay longer. No problem. Just give me, say, a twenty four hour heads up when you want to leave."

Cane couldn't help but curl his lips. "Thank you, I appreciate it."

"Not a problem." Cane turned to leave. "Oh, Mister Cane? Damn, I mean Emmett." He turned. "I need to know if you are being accompanied, for health and safety reasons?"

Cane looked to him. "Not at this moment. If I find the right property, or properties, I'll call in my business partner and have him come out here to take a look. Until then, though, I'm on my own."

## 2

Millers Fall was blessed when it came to emergency services. For a town of less than five hundred to have a patrol of thirteen full time police officers, its own fire department and an ambulance depot all within its borders, the township there felt more than happy with any emergency situation which might occur. Granted, the services served the neighbouring towns too, but having the HQ's gave its residents piece of mind for any situation.

Officer Diana Trent of the Millers Fall Police Department strolled inside the dispatch room at a little before eight, clutching a coffee purchased from the vending machine down the hall. The room housed six desks, each with a computer system, monitor, headset and telephone, ready for whatever The Fall would throw at them during the course of the moderate, May evening.

Another officer uttered something about kids outside McGinty's Bar in to his headset as she wandered by. He turned and whispered a silent 'hi,' raising his free hand in greeting. Diana extended the index finger that clutched her coffee and nodded back.

The briefing that night had been swift. A few kids playing pranks, probably what Clark was dealing with on the comms system she guessed, but nothing else. The missing boys were still on the list, but no new information had surfaced in a month. Nothing new gave them very little to work with.

Weekdays had a history of being more subdued than the Friday to Sunday morning shifts of the weekend.

Diana draped her coat over the back of a chair, placed the coffee on her desk and sat down, flashing a glance through the internal windows into the corridor. The lights didn't do much to battle the darkness out there, and with a clear, night sky broken by the solitary lot light outside, it looked like the monitor screens would provide the most illumination during the dark hours.

A few more officers waded in. Kim Nieman, the rookie who'd served about ten months or so, followed by Andrew Loveridge, the coolest officer on the beat, with his wavy hair pulled back in to a pony tail and finely trimmed beard, now something of a trademark around town.

"Damn nights," he said, slouching in the chair opposite.

Diana flashed a smile. "Could be worse. You could be on the beat. Forecast said heavy rain about two-ish." She watched as he yawned and nodded.

He cupped a fist in front of his mouth. "Wouldn't be so bad if I'd slept last night. Day. Whenever it was."

"Evening."

Diana looked up as Officer Alex Duggan passed by. He strolled to the desk in front and sat down.

"Hey," Andrew replied.

"Where's your partner in crime?" Kim asked, donning the headset.

"Getting knocked back from Jeanette again," he laughed.

"He still trying? Wow, that's determination. She should say yes just to shut him up." Diana recalled the soft spot Michael had for Jeanette Perry since she'd joined the force three years ago. And yep, he was still trying after all this time.

"Hey, here's our resident Romeo," Clark announced as Michael entered.

"Piss off," he smirked, taking the desk behind Diana. Andy looked across and lifted his brows. Diana turned back to her monitor with a smile. The line buzzed, signalling the first call of the shift. She reached across and took the call.

"Millers Fall dispatch, may I help you?"

"Yeah, I think so. I need to report some kind of, like a, disturbance or something?"

The calm but confused male voice engaged her attention.

"Okay. What is it I can help you with, sir?"

"Uh, listen, I don't want to sound like a crank or nothing, but I'm out walking my dog and I wandered in to the fog out here on Glenn Avenue. It looks like there's lightning or something, cracking through the area. I don't know if there's a power-line down, but there's some kind of electricity or something happening."

The voice was sincere. Diana knew from experience a hoax and the real deal.

"Through the area?" she enquired, beginning the first stage of the investigation.

"Yeah, I mean, not from the sky. It's actually at ground level. Like, in the road. You can see it flashing and hear the voltage. There's some kind of power-outage or something going on in there."

Diana frowned. "Okay, and are you safely away from the cable?"

"Yes, I got my dog tethered and we're way away from it."

"And is there anyone in immediate danger that you know of?"

Glenn Avenue was a stretch of tarmac leading out in to the countryside at the top end of town. A few homes clustered together on the outskirts, but the next dwelling was a mile and a half away.

"Not that I can see. The homes looked empty from what I can see."

"Sir, can you tell me your name, please?"

"Brian."

"Okay, Brian, I want you stay on the line. I'm going to contact the power company and see if there's a fault on the grid."

"No problem."

With the call held she opened a new line. "Anyone know who supplies the power to Glenn Avenue?"

Alex turned around. "Glenn Avenue? Try D-Power. They're in the directory. I think they're the biggest provider. Better to start with the big one and work your way through."

Diana opened the on-screen database and typed the company name in the search bar. "Got it." She clicked the number and listened as the dial tone in her ear began to ring. First, an automated female voice gave out the list of options available after hours. Diana chose the emergency option, and was answered within three rings.

"D-Power. How may I help you?"

The voice was male, and courteous. "Hi, this is officer Diana Trent from the Miller's Fall Police Department. I'm currently working in the dispatch room, and was wondering if I may speak with someone about a possible power surge or something which has been reported to us by a member of the public?"

"Well, that would be me. I'm working the emergency line tonight, ma'am."

"Thank you, sir. May I ask your name, please?"

"Dean Bareford, I'm an engineer here."

"Okay, Dean, as I said, we've had a complaint of a downed power-line or something to that effect on Glenn Avenue, a somewhat isolated residential road leading out of town. The gentleman reporting this incident has called in from the scene, and described, like, lightning flashing through the fog that's settling up there. I was wondering if there was a fault on the grid, a loss of power or something that you may be aware of that's causing this?"

"Let me just check for you." The tap from Dean's keyboard tinkled over the line. The flashing green light on the switchboard confirmed that Brian still held on the other. "Okay, I've got the power coverage we provide to Miller's Fall on my screen. We cover about, say, seventy percent of your area, and..." the keyboard tapped over the headset again, "yes; we cover Glenn Avenue and its occupants. There's another property about a mile and a half away from the cluster of customers we have on the outskirts, and that's not covered by any power company that I can see, so I can't feed any information from there."

"No, that's fine. The people in that property don't receive any power from what I know." From across the desks Alex answered an incoming call.

Dean continued over her ear-peace. "Right. I mean, yeah, looking at this, it seems that the power distribution along the road itself is as it should be. Everything's reading normal."

Diana frowned. "Oh, okay. There's no cuts, no disturbances at all?"

"No, not a thing. Not according to our grid. The properties are being supplied as they should be, and there's nothing out of the ordinary with our lines. Everything's running as it should be."

"That's strange. It's the only thing I could think of which could cause lightning at a low level, like the witness is reporting." From ahead, Alex muttered 'Glenn Avenue.'

"Well, I can assure you that there's no escape of power. You said there was fog out there? Is it possible your disturbance could be weather related? I mean, I'm no weatherman but maybe there's something in the atmosphere that could be causing this?"

"Yeah, that's what I'm thinking. The guy reporting this, though, believes everything is happening at ground level. I'm guessing the next thing to investigate is the weather, if everything your end is fine?"

"It is, Officer. There's no faults registering and there's nothing I can find visually that tells me that we have a problem."

"Okay, Mister Bareford, I appreciate your time. Thank you."

"No problem. I'll keep monitoring the area anyway, and if something happens I'll contact you."

"That's great. Have a pleasant evening. Thank you."

"Pleasure. Take care."

Diana cut the line and sighed. The green light continued to flash. Alex turned around and placed a note on her desk, simply reading 'lightning Glenn Ave.' He turned back before the pair could make eye contact. She studied his writing and pressed the switch back to the caller.

"Hello Brian?" she asked, somewhat surprised he'd held the line. "Brian?" The line hissed. No signs of life out there. "Brian, this is

Officer Trent from the dispatch room. Are you there?" No one replied. "Hello?" Andrew took a call opposite, his voice clearer than Alex's. Diana toyed with hanging up but her conscience held the upper hand. "Brian? Hello?"

"Hello?" Alex repeated. "Ma'am, are you still there?"

"Glenn Avenue?" Andrew questioned. "Hold the line one moment, sir." He closed the line. "I have a resident on Glenn Avenue reporting an electrical fault. What's going on?"

Diana shook her head. "I have no idea."

Alex turned on his chair. "I had a resident on the line reporting lightning outside her home in the fog. Line just went dead. Can't get her back. Nothing."

Diana released a small giggle, one bore of disbelief. "My line's still open. I have nothing but silence on the other end. The power company's registering no problems up there."

Andrew turned back to his desk. "I'll get someone on it."

"No, no. I'll do it. Just tell your call we're aware of the situation and dispatching." It was either nerves or excitement that passed through Diana as she took control of the situation. A mystery was afoot. The silence in her ear became deafening. Brian had either pulled a fast one or vanished. The whole situation, as corny as it sounded, was indeed a mystery.

"Sarge, are you getting all this?"

Across the headset Sargent Harris, the man responsible for this shift, was listening, hidden away in another room.

"Yeah, I got you, Diana. Keep doing what you're doing. Kim, contact the nearest weather centre and see if they're reporting anything out that way."

"Got it." Diana closed the Sergeant's line and opened another, patching through to a colleague she'd known for years and trusted more than anyone else. "Dispatch to car seventy seven, come in?"

After a moment a familiar voice responded. "Seventy seven to dispatch, go ahead."

"Hey Benny, listen, we've had a few calls come in reporting some kind of disturbance up on Glenn Avenue. Two of the callers hung up before we could finish-"

"Three," Andrew interrupted. "Mine's just cut, too."

"Make that three," Diana continued. "They all reported some kind of lightning in the fog that's forming up there. I thought maybe it was something to do with the lines, but the power company have confirmed no problems. Would you mind heading up and just checking it out for us?"

"No problem, Dee. You sure it just ain't Hoyt and his freaks messing around, stealing cable or something like that?"

"That's the thing, Ben. We have no real info on what it is. It may very well be his clan, family, whatever you want to call them, but we just don't know."

"I'd imagine he's got something to do with it. I'll head out now and see what's what."

Diana smiled to the monitor. "Thanks."

Kim, engaged in conversation, looked across, shaking her head. "Okay, thank you. Bye. Nothing. There's no lightning, no fog, nothing showing on their radars."

Alex frowned. "There has to be. The call I took said lightning in the fog."

"Me too. Fog and lightning," Andrew replied.

"What the hell is going on?" Diana stretched her arms in to the air.

"Millers Fall emergency dispatch. How my I help you?" Michael adjusted his headset as he took the call. "Okay, ma'am, I need you to calm down please.... okay, calm, I can't understand you.... right, and you are where in comparison?" His eyes jumped from the monitor for a second. "Do you know where he is? No ma'am, I.... yes, I am listening. I – Shit!" He winced, throwing the headset from his ear. "Damn it!"

"What?" Diana asked.

"Damn, Glenn Avenue. Geez." He prodded a finger inside his ear. "A woman, hysterical as hell, saying her husband vanished. Same as you guys had. Lightning. Fog, then this crazy, high pitched squeal that tore through my head. Damn that hurt."

Diana returned to her monitor. "Dispatch to car seventy seven, are you reading me?"

"Loud and clear, Diana. Making my way to Glenn now."

"Benny you have to be careful. Something's happening up there and we don't know what. Everyone who called in has gone silent. We don't know how dangerous the situation is."

"Copy that, Diana, I'm approaching with caution."

She turned to her colleagues. "See what other vehicles are operating tonight, please."

"It's okay. If anything rowdy's happening I'll call for backup," Benny replied across the radio. "I'm almost there."

Clark looked across to her. "We got vehicle twenty four and thirty six on the beat tonight. Without sirens their ETA will be three and five minutes respectively. They're patrolling the west and south." He poised on his head set, ready for Diana's call.

"Have them run out there, no sirens."

"Sure."

"Okay, I'm just turning on to Glenn now," Benny began, across the airwaves. "Damn, the fog is heavy out here. Hold on, wait a minute."

"What?" Diana snapped.

"I've got a member of the public flagging me down. He's running up now. Let me speak with him and I'll get back to you."

"Asap, Benny, that's an order." Clark looked across and gave a thumbs up, signalling the officers had been dispatched. "The vehicles are on their way," Diana said, relaying the message. "Stay safe."

"Will do."

Diana closed the line and stood, making her way between the desks to the map of Millers Fall pinned to the wall. Running a finger across its roads, she found Glenn Avenue.

"I'm guessing that Hoyt and his people are up to something," a different voice suggested. Diana turned to see Sergeant Harris enter the dispatch room. His bulky frame hung loose over a leather belt, forcing the shirt to expand to its capacity. His silver hair and crow's feet bore a career well experienced in the force, and one she knew had earned a desk job from which he often presided.

"I don't think so," she replied, turning to face him. "Hoyt and his, well, *family*, usually keep to themselves. In all the years I've lived in The Fall, I've never once seen or heard of them committing any crime."

"Brainwashing should be a crime. They all need to be locked up. Who knows what the hell they get up to out in those woods?" Harris perched his frame on the edge of Andrew's desk as Diana returned to hers.

"Guess we'll find out in a minute," Kim replied.

For a few moments the dispatch room fell in to silence, evoking a sense of discomfort to Diana. It was never this quiet in the dispatch room, not ever.

# 3

"Car twenty four to dispatch, come in dispatch." Finn Renton rode shotgun tonight in vehicle twenty four. At thirty five years of age, chiselled good looks and a body seemingly sculpted by Michaelangelo, he was the most eligible bachelor in The Fall. He wasn't muscular or skinny, but exactly in the middle where it's deemed most healthy men should aim to be. He released the button on the talk set and peered out in to the fog that was settling.

"This is dispatch," Diana's voice crackled from the speaker.

"Hey Diana, me and Max are just turning on to Glenn now. We'll contact you as soon as we know what's going on, over."

"Got it, Finn. Keep safe."

"Will do. Out."

Max laughed beside him. "You know, you don't have to do this whole military, professional, over and out crap when you're taking comms. We're just a small time department out here."

Finn guessed Max was twenty or so years older than him, give or take, and had been a country boy his whole life. His moustache engulfed the top lip, and if the horseshoe of hair around his head had not shared the same, darkened brown colour, he'd have guessed it was dyed.

"I can't help it, it just, sort 'a, comes out."

Through the fog the siren lights of Benny's car flashed red, then blue, one after the other. Max slowed to a standstill as the rear of the vehicle loomed in to view.

"Where is he?" Max asked, killing the engine.

Finn leaned forward, squinting through the windscreen. "I can't see him. His door's open, though."

"The driver door?"

"Yeah, looks like it."

Both men looked to each other before checking their standard issue Glock 22's were holstered. Finn rummaged under his seat for the flashlight he kept there. "Best go check it out," he said, turning the light on.

Finn stepped out in to the fog, shuddering at the rapid drop in temperature. He chilled in an instant, shivering as his body adjusted to the switch.

"Damn, it's cold," Max gasped as he stepped out.

Both men wandered across the road and toward the vehicle. Finn approached, aiming the flashlight inside the patrol car. He studied its interior, leaning to look through the rear window on the driver's side. The glare of light reflected from the glass and bounced back, creating bright spots that distorted his vision. It was empty. Ben was a stickler for tidiness, and never let his vehicle soil with wrappers or cups like some on the force did. No track signalled he'd left the car. There was no sign of confrontation. Finn shone the light back and forth, but knew he wouldn't find anything. The handset for the officer's radio sat on the driver's seat.

The sound of an approaching car broke the silence. The vehicle stopped, allowing officer's Tina Sheridan and Oscar LaFondra to join them.

"You find him?" Tina asked as they approached. She'd been the smart one to wear the standard issue black jacket.

"Just got here," Finn replied, standing upright. "From what I can see, no, we haven't."

LaFondra brought to life his own flashlight and scoured the vehicle. "He couldn't have got far," he began, "he was talking to dispatch just a few minutes ago."

Tina joined her partner in examining Ben's vehicle. "Maybe he's up at one of the houses?" she asked, sounding unsure.

"Okay, here's what we'll do." Max was the oldest and most experienced member on the force. Finn usually stepped back and allowed him to deliver direction whenever it was needed. Usually,

Max was right, and Finn never doubted him. "Finn and I will take the properties on the right side of the road, if you both take the left. Let's just knock the doors, see if he's in there, and reassure the public we have the situation under control."

"What if we don't find him?" LaFondra asked.

"Let's just see what we turn up, then we'll deal with anything else we might need to."

Finn parted from Max as they crossed the road, veering to the right, Max the left. From the fog a detached house appeared. A porch covered the ground floor of the home at the main entrance, and Finn noted the boards creaking as he skipped up the steps. *'Knock knock,'* he thought, before placing four knocks upon the door. He stood, looking around whilst waiting to be answered. Across the way echoed the same four knocks, this time from next door. Finn stood on tiptoes then back to his soles. After a moment he knocked again. The cold was stabbing at every opportunity, and deciding there would be no answer, he began inspecting the property. The lights were on in the first window. He peered in through the open curtains and noted the TV playing away to itself. *Ghost Adventures*, if he wasn't mistaken. The lounge, otherwise, was deserted. Finn tapped the window. "Hello? Anyone in? It's the Millers Fall Police Department. Hello?"

It was clear no-one would respond. The TV, still playing, suggested a quick getaway for its owners, like a medical emergency or something. Diana had said something about more than one call coming in from this neck of the woods.

Jumping down the porch with a single stride, Finn made his way through the fog, guided by his flashlight. He met Max at the neighbour's gate. "Anything?" he asked.

Max shook his head. "Nope. No one home."

"Me either."

Finn reached down and took the radio holstered to his waist. "This is Renton to dispatch, come in dispatch?"

The speaker fluttered with interference, sounding greater in the quiet street, before falling silent.

"Battery dead?" Max asked, reaching for his own.

"Shouldn't be." Finn shook the handset, like this would re-energise the radio somehow. "I can't believe for one second it would be released for duty with no charge?"

Max raised his brows. "Stranger things have happened."

"Damn it." Finn looked about, noticing a flashlight approaching.

"Call to dispatch, come in dispatch." Max attempted to make contact via his own comms.

"Got an empty house over there," Tina stated as she joined them.

Finn nodded. "Same here. I got the TV going but no-one to watch it."

"You gain entry?"

"No, just saw through the window."

"Call to dispatch, come in dispatch." Max growled at his handset.

"What's up?" Tina asked.

Max waved the radio in Finn's direction. "Finn got a shit load of interference on his. I'm seeing if I can reach dispatch instead."

"Anything?" Finn asked, but already knew the answer.

"Not a damn thing. Not even the damned interference you did. Mine's just dead, well and truly."

Tina tried her radio, achieving the same results. The three stood there, silhouetted against the mist, briefly appearing human when the siren lights flashed across them. They tried the car radios in each vehicle, but again could not reach out to their colleagues back at the station.

"What the hell is going on?" Finn asked after they'd exhausted all communication devices. Even the cells had no signal.

"This is just plain weird if you ask me," Max replied.

"Oscar," Tina added.

Finn looked over his shoulder. "Yeah. Where is he?"

"Oscar?" Max shouted. The fog had thickened while they busied themselves, smothering all but the closest lights.

Tina peered at the element. "Look at this. When did it become so foggy?"

Finn shivered, recognising another temperature drop.

"Oscar?" Max asked once more. The gentle breeze directing the cloud offered the only response. Apart from that, it was silent. No vehicles in the distance. No farm animals from the fields surrounding them, and no birds tweeting from the hidden tree tops.

Finn un-holstered the handgun. "First Ben and now Oscar? Don't tell me nothing's going on up here."

Tina and Max followed suit. "You see which way he went?" Max asked her.

"Yeah. The house up from me."

Max moved closer. "All three of us stick together. We're the only ones out here. We got no back up if anything happens, understand? We have to be on our game."

For the first time in his Miller County career, Finn became anxious. "Yes," he replied, as the thump in his chest became more noticeable.

Max led the way, his handgun outstretched. Finn followed with Tina. From ahead, the fog began to swirl. It circled as though attempting to hypnotise the approaching officers. Max held out a hand. Finn and Tina stopped. The fog swirled quicker, its edges disbanding in to strands. From its core an orange light began to flicker. Blasts of air attacked them, pushing them backward. They stumbled and stuttered, attempting to keep balance. The light exploded, bathing its surroundings like a summer sunset.

"Oscar?" Finn asked, noting its similarity to a flashlight. "Ben?"

Max stumbled back. The swirl groaned, rumbling the road underfoot and quaking the ground. The fog pulled back, revealing the horror they were now doomed to endure. "God almighty!" Max wailed. Tina screamed. Finn looked to the gun in his hand. The terror he witnessed would stain his mind forever, an image from which he could never escape. The barrel placed between his eyes, but it was too late. The gun had been rendered obsolete. The trigger squeezed beneath his finger again, again and again, but the cartridge did not fire. Finn screamed, turning back to the swirl. Horrendous images greeted him. Finn covered his eyes, frozen with fear, and prayed for death to come quickly.

***

"What time is it?" Harris asked, attempting to raise any one of the officers out on Glenn.

"Almost midnight," Michael replied.

Diana sat back in her chair, gravely worried for her colleagues. Something was wrong, and wrong in the most dreadful sense of the word. Police were often ribbed for their hunches, but Diana had that gut feeling. She felt it. Something was seriously, seriously wrong. Chewing a nail she looked to her colleagues. Their concern was clear, too.

Sergeant Harris' voice became intense. She guessed his anger disguised some kind of nervousness. "This is Sergeant Harris to any officer patrolling Millers Fall. Come in."

Alex rose from his chair. "I'm going to head out, see if I can find them."

"I'll join you." Michael stood, pushing his chair out as he did so.

"My God! Look at this!" Kim bolted to her feet and peered out the window.

Andy joined her. "What the...."

Shadows from the open blinds appear in the room as a light emerged outside. The officers forgot their tasks and looked out across The Fall, only now it wasn't night. The sky burned orange, hiding all but the brightest of stars. It intensified and illuminated, as though ablaze from both horizons. As Diana watched, the midnight hour became a hazy, summer day, bathing the buildings and trees outside in a vibrant, orange glow. The daylight lasted a short while, burning above for all to see. People from nearby buildings ran on to the sidewalk in their pyjamas and stood, mesmerised, by the strange phenomenon. Dogs barked in unison, alerting their owners to the skies alteration. Clouds drifted by, swirling in various patterns, as though a thousand breezes expanded in different directions. Millers Fall bathed within light from every border. The sky was strange, but pleasant, and although it confused Diana, she looked to it in awe.

"What is this?" Clark asked, sounding a million miles away. None of the officers answered the calls coming through to the switchboard.

"An eclipse or something?" Michael suggested.

Sergeant Harris wandered to the head of the group. "I have no idea...."

As mysterious as it started, the summer sky began to dim. It faded, back down to the horizon, and left The Fall in the darkness it was accustomed to at this hour.

The officers did not move. "What did I just witness?" Andrew asked, to no particular person. No-one, not even Diana, answered him.

**4**

Diana sat at home. She'd attempted to enjoy her day off, but five missing colleagues and the Feds arriving at The Fall disrupted her plans. She owned the flat above Denny's Groceries, which sat in the middle of a tee junction. If she peered out the window to her left, the small shops began, and away to her right they finished. Ahead, her view of the surrounding woodland was blocked by the elementary school, but all in all it didn't bother her. The Fall was arguably the quietest town in America, probably the world. The only thing she ever heard, when not on duty on a Saturday night, was her cat fighting with another on the sidewalk.

She shared her flat with Drake, the feline in question. He'd been named after the lead character in her favourite book, *Haunted*, written by some English author she'd never heard of until reading it. Drake now curled in her lap and purred with content. As much as Diana tried to concentrate on other things, her mind wandered back to the events of last night. How could five, armed police officers vanish? There was talk of Mitchum Hoyt in the station before she left this morning. Hoyt was a strange one. Not short of money, he owned the farm on the outskirts of town, deep in the woodland of the county. Hoyt was seen as something of a cult leader amongst the residents of Millers Fall, harbouring a number of people on his property who believed what he preached in.

Hoyt had been known to predict everything from the end of the world to the second coming. Some people believed him, word for word, and chose to live on his property out there in the backwoods. Spurning society, they lived peacefully in the middle of nowhere. Diana had been on the force for over a decade, and not once did any issues surface from Mitchum Hoyt or his followers. From time to time they made their way in to town, but kept away from the public for the most part, choosing to live a quiet existence in their own company.

The vibration of the cell phone returned Diana to reality. The caller ID informed her that the station was attempting to get through.

"Hello?"

"Diana? It's Sergeant Harris."

"Hi, Sarge."

"Diana, listen, I don't suppose you can do me a favour? Can you come in and cover a few hours this evening, six 'til ten, please? The Sheriff's got the Feds in, and we are seriously, seriously understaffed after, you know, last night."

Diana thought a moment. At least if she was on duty she could stay in the loop somewhat, instead of mulling things in her mind with no-one to talk to.

"Yeah. Yes, that's fine. I'll be with you soon."

"That's great, Diana. I owe you. Thanks."

"No worries. See you soon."

Diana hung up and tapped the phone against her teeth. She stood, forgetting where Drake was sleeping, and launched the squealing cat across the lounge.

# 5

Cane sat at the table, looking in to the parking lot though the window. That sunset was something else. He'd never seen the likes of that before, at least not at that time of day. A potato chip crunched between his teeth, sending crumbs down to the papers he waded through. After spending the evening at Ellie's, eating burgers and making friends, he'd found the location of the town library. First thing that morning he'd jumped in the car and headed down there. Millers Fall lived up to its reputation. He'd seen about fifteen cars at rush hour along the busiest street. Once there, he set himself at a desk and examined the archives. Nothing much happened in The Fall until two boys vanished, which itself only occurred a few months ago. This was what he wanted, and without arousing suspicions, printed the articles to bring back and study. He'd listened to the drab of people sloping in and out, all commenting on the night sky. The librarian must have been sick of it by the time he left.

He wiped crumbs from the paper with a swift palm. "Town boys listed missing. Families plea for safe return. The strange Mitchum Hoyt. I think I'm on to something." He swiped the dictaphone and pressed 'record'. "Mitchum Hoyt appears to be a focal point of this town's plight. I'll have to find out where he is without drawing any attention." If a stranger just appears in town asking questions about some guy they all point the finger to, soon everyone will be looking at him, or at least that was his thought.

Cane scanned the reports. Brent Peterson and Jason Wight, two names that reoccurred in every article. They'd been missing since March, and not a police force in the area had any idea where to find them. No eyewitnesses, no leads, no nothing. They we're kids. Cane guessed it was a successful escape from family life at first, but the more he read, the more one name lifted from the pages and changed his mind.

"Mitchum Hoyt. I need to find him." He slumped in the chair, rubbing his eyes.

"He won't be difficult to locate. The reports suggest a farm on the outskirts of town. Shadow Oak Farm," he told the device. "If these reports hold an ounce of truth, it's gonna be guarded in some way. The way they read makes him sound like some kind of new age Charles Manson." The dictaphone dropped to the desk. "I'll take a trip out there tonight."

\*\*\*

"Okay, this is what I want you to do." Diana partnered with Clark, for this evening at least. Harris offered a quick briefing out in the parking lot. "I want you to head over there and just see if anything strange was happening last night. See if they noticed anyone on their property, or if they know anything about what happened."

"Even if they do, they're not going to say much," Clark replied.

Sergeant Harris opened his hands. "If they don't, they don't. But at least we'll have an indication of if they're involved somehow."

"Sounds like you think they are," Diana stated from across the vehicle.

Harris smiled. "You never know with them. Just go see what you can find." Diana slumped in to shotgun as Clark took charge behind the wheel. Harris looked over his shoulder as he walked away. "And let Diana do the talking."

"What's wrong with me?" Clark asked.

"Sometimes you're a real ass, Clark. Let Diana do the talking."

\*\*\*

They turned off of Glenn Avenue at a little after eight, as the daylight dwindled. In all honesty, there had been very little daylight beforehand anyway, as the clouds formed and the thunder stalked the county from the far reaches of the horizon. Every now and then a distant rumble emerged through Diana's window.

They'd taken an alternative route leading on to Glenn Avenue, as the Sheriff and Feds had cautioned off the residential area both ways after the disappearance last night. They hadn't heard anything official from the crime scene, but rumour had it that a day of forensic testing had revealed nothing.

Clark slowed the vehicle as he approached the turning to Hoyt's farm. Diana noticed the dark, foreboding sky, where the road and fields merged. A storm approached. The patrol car turned and made acquaintance with a track, not nearly as smooth as the tarmac they'd just left. The vehicle bounded across the uneven surface, rocking the officers from side to side. They entered an avenue of evergreens sprawling out as far as they could see on both sides. Not far in, Diana caught the scent of fresh pine through her window. Thunder clapped in the distance. Lightning flickered beyond the trees.

"I hope to God we don't get the rain until after we're done," Clark began as he navigated the woodland floor, "there's no way I'm staying out here if this track gets washed out."

The darkness of the distant woodland appeared between the trunks. It was a darkness you just knew could not be penetrated, even by a blazing, summer sun. Now, in this light, things were starting to get creepy.

"Me either."

The track continued for half a mile or so, until they reached a simple, wooden gate. Illuminated in the headlights a hand-painted sign read 'Private Property'.

Clark stopped the vehicle. "Guess we continue on foot."

Diana left the car and joined her partner at the farm's boundary. The track underfoot was pretty solid, and would take a lot of rain before messing with the patrol car's tyres. Ahead, the dilapidated farmhouse they journeyed to loomed from the dwindling light. A porch in its middle flanked by windows either side made the front of the house. The first storey was similar, with more windows stretched across the face. The sloping roof, even in this light, appeared in need of some renovation, with a few gaps dotted here and there. The entire building was covered in white slats, although many were weathered and broken. The entire structure looked like something from a post apocalypse movie.

A rusted tractor took residence on a patch of grass, forming a small barrier between them and the building. To the left of the home a huge pile of logs had been chopped, and presumably ready for use. Away, in the distance to the right, smaller buildings similar to the home existed. From the farmhouse, orange light appeared in most windows.

"Looks like someone's home," Clark noted, placing his hands on the gate's frame.

The tingle of nerves passed through Diana. Never once had she been apprehensive whilst working the beat in Millers Fall, but there was always going to be a first time, and that time was now.

"May I help you?"

Diana jumped as a strong, southern accent emanated from the darkness. She turned to see a lamp approaching. As it drew closer, the huge frame of a bearded man appeared. Illuminated by flame, he wore faded jeans and a dirty, white vest. A black and red chequered shirt draped from his shoulders. Strands of cotton frayed where its arms once existed.

"Ah, yes. Yes you may," Clark began as the figure approached. Diana looked up as he came to a standstill. The guy was huge. She guessed about six foot nine, maybe ten. From his left hand hung three, lifeless rabbits.

Remembering Sergeant Harris' orders, Diana interrupted her partner, and hoped to God her nervousness didn't show. "Hi, we're with the Millers Fall Police Department."

"I can see that. What do you want?"

Diana startled at the bluntness of his reply. The beard emerging from his face had to be a foot long. She was no expert on male hair growth, but the black bristles must have been untended for at least a year or so.

"We would like to speak with a Mister Mitchum Hoyt, please."

"About what?"

This time, Clark did the interrupting. "Sir, we're here on official police business, it'd be best if you co-operated."

Diana expelled a sight and looked upward. It was all about the power with him.

The figure smiled in the lamplight. "Is that so?"

"Yes, it is. Please, don't make this any worse than it is."

Diana turned and flashed her partner a glare.

"Well, let me tell you something, *sir*," the bearded man began, "I believe I have the right to refuse you entry to our property. After all, it's private, as it clearly states on that sign. Second, if this was anything more than just a routine call, you'd have a warrant and be on this side of the gate without asking for any kind of permission. Also, you haven't flapped a piece of paper at me, so I know damn well you can't exercise your full force right here, right now." The man cackled, which, due to his size, became a bellow. "So, I see it that I have two choices. One, I can send you packing back to The Fall, tell you to go bring back your warrant, which will take you a while. Or, as I see it, you can remember your manners, you're please and thank you's, show a little respect for us, what, wild folk is it? Or cult? Something like that? Anyhow, you approach me with good graces and I'll see what I can do to help you. What do you say?"

"That's absolutely fine, Mister, uh?" Diana took the lead again before Clark could screw this up, too.

"Altman. Everyone calls me Altman."

"Mister Altman. Your right, we're just out to see if anything strange happened here last night?"

Altman laughed again. "Ma'am, there's always something strange happening around here."

Diana thought as much. "Okay, well, anything that you're not used to? We have five missing officers and six families, all from the outskirts of The Fall, just down the road."

Altman's face dropped, expressing an immediate anger. "What you trying to say?"

Anxiety surged in to her being.

"Nothing, we're not saying anything," Clark chipped in. "We're going round all the properties in the area to see if anyone noticed anything unusual. For example, last night we have eyewitness accounts of heavy fog and strange lights at this end of town. We just want to see if you can help us with some information, that's all."

Altman looked them over. His expression suggested a conflict of trust.

"That's all," Diana said in a soft tone, confirming Clark's explanation.

"You're not gonna try and take us away? Or interfere in our way of life?"

Diana shook her head and smiled. "No, Mister Altman, not at all."

"Alright. You wait here. I'll come get you if he says so."

Altman trudged away across the grass and past the tractor.

Clark sighed. "That was tense."

Diana nodded. "Yep. It was."

"I had a hand on my holster. I thought he was gonna attack."

"Well, he didn't. Seems like he's more worried about what we will do to this place, if anything."

"Well, you have to admit; it's a bit freaky living this deep in the woods with countless others. Who knows what goes on here?"

Diana turned to him. "You ever think maybe nothing?"

Clark shrugged. "Maybe."

"Perhaps they just want to live in peace, away from the rat race and pressure of modern life?"

"Perhaps. Or, perhaps they're attempting to raise Satan?"

"Come in!" Altman called from the porch.

Clark sighed again. "Here goes."

\*\*\*

Diana stepped inside the dilapidated hallway. The gloom broke only by candles that littered on top of a small table, and inside holders perched upon the walls. Her footsteps echoed as she moved across floorboards, feeling like she'd entered a newly acquired project home instead of a home fit to live. To her left a staircase ran upward, its floorboards warped and exposed. At the bottom step a door rested, slightly ajar. From the darkness more amber light appeared. A corridor ran away to the right, parallel to the staircase. Two more doors, one close, one at the end, hung from hinges, unfixed for a while it seemed. Cobwebs danced in a hidden breeze between the banisters and from an unused light shade. The musty smell of dereliction hung heavy about them.

"Wait here," Altman ordered, closing the door behind Clark. He wandered away along the corridor with heavy footfalls. Thunder rumbled from outside, louder now as it rolled closer.

Clark whispered, moving closer. "Which room do you think belongs to Leatherface?"

Diana tutted. "Cut it out."

Her curiosity began to take over, and she moved to the stairs. In the hallway, looking down, American Gothic stared back. In the strange light, with shades of darkness at its edges, the farmer almost looked real. From a distance, music played. Then, to Diana's ear, the sound of conversations emerged from different directions. There was no way to pinpoint them, but many of the voices appeared distressed.

"You hear that?" Clark asked, still whispering.

Diana nodded, examining the surroundings. "Yeah. Yeah, I do."

"What the hell is going on here?"

"I have no idea."

The tell-tale sound of Altman's feet returned. "This way," he ordered, appearing from the shadows.

Clark looked to Diana. "Ladies first."

She rolled her eyes and headed toward the guide, who still clasped his lamp. Voices became clearer as she approached the farthest door, and through the gap noticed a man, curled over on his knees. Lumps on his spine protruded as he lurched forward, bathed in candle light. He sobbed in to his hands. "Forgive me. Forgive me," he cried, heartbroken and distressed.

"Hey!" Altman's voice blasted, causing her to jump. "This is not for outsiders to see." He stomped past and slammed the door shut. "Now, follow me."

Diana followed the giant along another corridor. At the end stood a single, wooden door. Altman knocked twice and opened. He nodded toward the room. Diana complied and brushed past in to a dark but spacious opening. In the corner, a small, round table housed a cluster of candles, their light failing to escape from much of their surroundings. A simple, felt chair with large arms sat before a bay window, looking out in to the surrounding woodland. Beside it, another table stood, holding an old grammar phone. The trumpet expelled *Summertime* by Sam Cooke. The crackle of the vinyl popped as the song played away. The closing door sealed their intentions. Altman had gone, leaving Clark alongside her in the room.

"Certainly is a fine night to admire Mother Nature's purest energy," a southern, distressing voice emerged. Diana turned back to the chair. Now used to the gloom, she could make out the form of someone peering out in to the wilderness. "When I was a child, my Daddy told me the thunder was God and his angels doing their spring cleaning, so that I wouldn't be afraid."

The thunder rumbled. A bolt of lightning flashed across the sky. Diana felt compelled to answer.

"As a good a story as I have heard."

A quaint laugh responded. "It sure was, and it did the job, too. I was no longer afraid, and from that day onward, I came to admire the lightning and the sound booming from the heavens."

Diana nodded, unable to answer. She looked across her shoulder to Clark, who shrugged.

"I believe, from Mister Altman's statement, that you've not ventured all the way out here to talk about the weather with me, have you, Miss?"

"No, no we haven't. I'm Officer Trent, this is Officer Parker. We're from the Millers Fall Police Department."

"The pleasure is all mine."

For whatever reason, Diana became a burden with nerves. Be it the dark, the setting, the warbling voices in the distance or the haunting melody of the music, her anxiety flourished.

"How should I address you, sir?" she asked.

"Officer, you may call me whatever you so wish. My name is Mitchum Hoyt, but feel free to call me Mitchum."

"Okay, *Mitchum*, thank you."

"Now, please tell me how I may help you good officers of the law?"

Diana found herself fumbling through a notepad. "We're out here to ask if anything out of the ordinary may have occurred in the area last night?"

"Officer Trent, there's always something out of the ordinary occurring out here at night." The echo of Altman's statement not ten minutes before.

"Well, you see, we're investigating a number of incidents that occurred yesterday. We have six family's missing from the outskirts of town and five armed police officers."

"Don't forget the sky," Mitchum added. The summer sky that burned through the darkness with an orange light had been classed a natural occurrence by the Millers Fall police.

"We are not currently worried about the atmospheric events of last night," Clark replied.

Hoyt's voice dropped. "Oh, but you should be." His tone became malevolent.

"What? Why should we be worried?" Diana asked, diverting from her questions.

"It's a sign. Nothing more and nothing less, at this moment in time, but you should heed it. Your townsfolk should heed it."

The passion and intensity in which he spoke brought another bout of anxiety to Diana. "If we could return to the questions I have, please?"

"By all means."

"We are asking everyone in the area if they noticed our officers or anyone else, or if they have any information that could possibly help us in our investigation?"

The head in the chair shook from side to side. "You're the first visitors we've had here for the best part of a year. Contrary to what the town believes, we do not kidnap people and brainwash them to accept our beliefs. You have my absolute blessing to search my entire premises to locate your missing people, but rest assured, where they went it's unlikely they'll come back the same."

"You know where they are?" Clark asked, stepping forward.

"Beyond the darkness my good man, beyond the darkness." Hoyt chuckled.

Thunder rattled the building.

"Tell me where they are!"

"Clark!" Diana snapped.

"This interview is over."

"Like hell it is!" Clark shouted.

"Dammit, Clark! Shut, up!"

"Feel free to search my farm, but please leave me. Now."

Diana restrained Clark as he moved to the chair. "Hoyt! Tell me where they are!"

"Am I suspected of committing a crime, officers?"

"No, Mister Hoyt, you are not," Diana responded.

"Then there is nothing more I have to say."

The door creaked. Both officers turned. Altman appeared, joined by another, larger man, with a similar long beard and shoulder length hair draped across his face. A woman accompanied them, clad in a dress that appeared from the turn of the century. They stared with eyes that harboured intention.

"I will ask you again, officers, please leave my property, now."

"Alright. Thank you for your cooperation, Mister Hoyt."

"Officer Trent, you may call me Mitchum."

Diana pushed Clark toward the door where Altman and his gang departed.

"Officers, one more thing." Diana turned back to the chair. Peering around it, for the first time, appeared Mitchum Hoyt. Long, straggly hair covered his bulbous face. A beard as long and unkempt as Altman's protruded in to the air. He smiled. "Remember my warning. Look to the sky, for it will burn. It will rage. You have been warned."

Hoyt laughed. A maniacal, terrifying laugh accompanied them along the corridor and out of the house.

The car appeared where they left it, intact and ready to go.

Diana wandered back and forth, one hand on her hip, the other on her forehead. "You gotta get yourself under control." She could have gained more info from Hoyt, and knew it.

"Yeah, I know. Look, I'm sorry, alright? I don't know what came over me. There's something about that house that just, well, made me feel nervous, or something. The atmosphere just wasn't right in there, and I didn't like it."

Diana placed both hands on her hips. "I know. I felt something, too. Something definitely isn't right in there."

"You think he's lying about our missing people?"

I don't know, but he gave us permission to search the place. I bet my bottom dollar when we report this back that a search warrant will be issued up here."

"Yes, then we'll know exactly what's going on."

Diana made her way toward the passenger side. "Come on, let's head back. I really need a coffee."

Clark smiled. "Just a coffee? Man, I think I need a change of underwear."

# 6

The portable TV played away to itself illuminating the darkened bedroom. The walls vanished behind an abundance of posters. A model TIE Fighter and Millennium Falcon suspended from the ceiling. A life-size Jason Voorhees stood against the bedroom door. Above the TV, an original *Return of the Jedi* lobby poster flashed within the intermittent light. Tad's father had managed to buy this for him whilst on a business trip, and he'd worshipped it ever since.

Tad looked at his alarm clock. It would be Saturday within half an hour. Time flies when you're having fun. In typical Tad Williams fashion, he'd told his parents he was doing his homework just so they'd agree to let him stay up and watch a movie. Currently, he was tapping out a conversation on his cell phone via Facebook. Billy Weiss and Jake Matthews were attempting to gain fake ID's, and a discussion was taking place over what job they should declare before sending twenty bucks and the completed form away. His laptop flashed in the darkness, and he looked to see Billy skyping him.

Tad moved across and sat on his desk chair, answering the call. Jake was already added to the conversation. He looked as both friends appeared in separate boxes on screen.

"Tad. How you doing?" Billy asked. His plump face and curly hair filled most of the screen. Jake looked the opposite, with his glasses reflecting the laptop's glare. *'My God,'* Tad thought, looking at them both, *'we really are the geek squad.'*

"Yeah, not bad. I see you both arguing over the fake ID's?"

"Right," Jake began. "I'm trying to explain to Billy that these ID's are gonna need realistic jobs added to them, to be taken seriously. Being the CEO of a marketing company just isn't going to be believable."

"And you two think that an ID saying you're both over twenty one, is?"

"Hell yeah!" Billy stated. "Look, I have a suit. My parents got it for me to wear at my Grandma's funeral, right? So, I go in Denny's, wearing a suit, pick up a six pack and take it to the counter. When he asks for my ID I produce the card, whilst wearing my finest. Its foolproof I tell 'ya, Tad. Sewn up and done."

"Okay, there's three things that you guys haven't considered, and these three things will end up biting you in the ass. One, you're both thirteen years old. Two, Denny has known all of us since we were born, and knows we're nowhere near to the legal drinking age, and three; Denny's is the only store in Millers Fall to sell liquor. You ever think that maybe your plan is just a little bit flawed?"

"I didn't think of that," Billy replied. "Way to crush my dreams, man."

"Where are you guy's getting this ID from, anyway?"

"The back of a magazine."

Jake sighed. "I think 'Operation Get-Shit-Faced' is gonna need more planning."

"Hey. Hey! Assmaster!" Tad turned to his bedroom door as Sam, his older brother, poked his head in.

"What?"

"Look what I got." Sam produced a handful of DVD's. Horror, action, and, of course, girlie ones.

"Where did you get them from?"

"They're in the trash behind Zuco's Entertainment. Looks like he's getting new stock or something? Me and Lance are the only ones who know they're out back. There's hundreds of them, just for the taking. Unlucky for you I guess. Everyone will know about it by tomorrow."

"Let me have some."

"Not a chance, geek-boy. You'll have to wait until tomorrow, but I'm gonna post and tweet they're all in there tonight. Don't worry, I'll tag you in it."

"I'll tell Mom and Dad."

"Go for it. I've still got that video of you and your little bitch friends trying to smoke. Remember that?" Tad fell silent. "Besides, you think Mom or Dad will do anything about it? Anyway, think I'll watch one of my newly acquired DVD's first then let everyone know where to find them. The only thing left for you tomorrow will be *Wild Wild West* and *Battleship*. Goodnight, fuctard." Sam laughed as he closed the door.

"What was that all about?" Billy asked as Tad returned to the screen.

"Sam. Man, he's an asshole."

"What's he done?" Jake enquired.

"Down behind Zuco's he found a dumpster full of DVD's. He wouldn't give me any and said he's gonna Facebook everyone about it after watching one. He's an asshole. He's just doing it to piss me off."

"Wait a minute. He's watching one first?" Tad saw the cogs behind Billy's lurch in to motion.

"That's what he said."

"Well why don't we get down there before he does it?"

"What?" Jake began, "there's no way I'd be allowed out at this time of night!"

"Ah, come on, Jake! None of us would be allowed out right this very minute. So what do we do? We bust out!"

"Yeah! Come on, Jake. I've busted out of here loads of times. The porch is below my window. We all have bikes. We can meet at the intersection; it wouldn't take more than fifteen minutes to be there and back." Tad escaped his prison a few times in the past, and to this day his parents were none the wiser.

"I don't know."

"Hey, to hell with it. I'll be at the intersection in ten minutes, and Tad will be with me. I'm gonna get me some of those Playboy DVD's if they're in."

"That's right, Jake. You're either with us or against us." Tad felt the surge of excitement.

"I swear you guys will be the death of me. Look, I'll do what I can."

Billy took charge. "Be there in ten minutes. I'm not waiting."

## 7

"Trent. Barton. Get in here," the Sheriff's voice called from his office. Glass windows separated the rest of the station from his private workspace. Diana looked across as he beckoned behind the open blinds. Leading Clark across the unusual bustle of the Police Department, she did as requested and entered the office. "Close the door."

Sheriff Mason Palmer served in the department his entire working life. Now, at a little north of fifty, he looked surprisingly good for a career full of drama and stress. He was no oil painting, at least not in Diana's eye, but a slim build, five o'clock shadow and only a hint of grey in that dark hair, she could tell he looked after himself. He gestured to two seats in front of his desk. "Take a seat."

Both officers did as they were asked, and as Palmer sat in his chair, introduced two men sat to their left. "Agent Davis and Welsh of the Federal Bureau of Investigation."

Diana nodded across to them. "Hello." Davis smiled. His heavily pitted skin told the story of an acne-ridden youth.

Palmer leant back in his seat. "So, what did you find out at Shadow Oak Farm?"

"Nothing of note," Clark began, "some weird goings on up there, but nothing illegal, at least not from what we saw."

"Clark's right. We didn't learn anything we didn't already know about them. It's a dark and dingy place, they live by candlelight and don't seem to know anything about our missing people. Well, not that they would disclose it, anyway. Hoyt offered us to search his premises if we wanted." Diana recalled his laugh echoing through the darkness and shuddered.

Agent Welsh leaned in to the conversation. "What do you think? You think they're hiding something?" Diana looked to him. "It's not a trick question, Officer."

'Here we go,' she thought. 'They haven't been here five minutes and already dick sizes are being used.'

"I think he's hiding something, but what I'm unsure. He said something real strange. Gave us some ramblings about the sky, and to warn the town. Weird stuff." She shrugged. "He's just a strange guy."

Sheriff Palmer frowned. "Does he mean the sky last night? It seems a little bit dramatic for an atmospheric disturbance."

"I don't know, sir. He spoke in riddles, and about things that didn't make sense. Mother Nature, not forcing anyone to join his family, things like that. He's just a strange individual, and those who follow him don't seem much better."

"You think he's worth pursuing?" Clark asked.

"Yes, I believe he's top of our list right now. He's the only option we haven't exhausted in the missing boys case, and you appear to have left with more questions than answers."

"You think he knows about the boys?" Agent Davis asked, turning to the Sheriff.

"He has to gain followers somehow."

"Someone should just tell him about Twitter," Clark quipped. Palmer flipped a glare that sent Clark's gaze straight to the floor.

"We'll start first thing," the Sheriff began. "I'll get Deputy Brooks up there with a squad and search warrant, then we'll see if we need to take any further action."

# The Kids 2354

"Hurry up, man!" Billy's voice echoed through the deserted street. He sat atop a black pushbike with a hood drawn tight. Jake sat beside him on a bike similar. Both looked as Tad approached.

"I'm coming!" he snapped, recalling the operation it took to escape his bedroom window to the porch roof, then to the garage to collect his bike. Neither of his parents had been alerted, and Sam was likely too engrossed in his titty DVD's to even care. Still, his annoyance at such a short time frame bugged him enough to rush the escape, which could have ended in his hasty recapture.

As a last minute thought, Tad grabbed his rucksack to maximise carrying power, and felt it slide across his back whilst peddling toward the crew.

He arrived under the streetlight on the junction. The town had died from the daily rigmarole. Even the surrounding houses showed little sign of life.

Billy tapped the screen of his iPhone. "No posts yet."

"Check his Twitter," Tad replied. The brakes squeezed beneath his fingers, screeching the tyre as he came to a standstill.

Billy swiped and tapped the screen, his face illuminating in the phones light. "No. I bet he's too busy fapping to Playmate of the Year."

"Let's get there while he is and make sure we get the good stuff before anyone else," Jake chipped in.

Billy looked at the backpack while shoving his phone inside the loose tracksuit pocket hanging from his thigh. "Damn, Tad. How many you taking?"

Tad smiled. "Enough to sell at school."

"Man's a genius," Jake sighed.

Tad changed the subject to something he'd thought about whilst biking over. "You do know there's likely to be patrol cars out tonight, with those people vanishing and all?"

Jake nodded. "Yeah. And we're gonna be heading up near Glenn Avenue. I heard police were all over there today."

"Don't worry about it," Billy replied, "we just stick to the dark. We see the police coming we head in to the parks. The back of Zuco's will be dark anyway. How else would Sam have got those DVD's?"

Billy had a point. Millers Fall was full of open space, parks and recreation grounds. The biggest challenge would be Glenn Avenue, That's if the police presence was as heavy as they believed.

"May I take this opportunity to suggest we get a move on, gentlemen? Time's ticking." Jake pointed to his watch.

Billy released a grunt of amusement. "Jake, it's no wonder we get our asses kicked for hanging with you."

"Trust me, fellas. You're biggest ass-kicking is yet to come, mark my words." Jake pushed his bike around and peddled away. "Tally-ho!"

Tad looked to Billy. "Who the hell says 'tally-ho' anymore?"

"That guy."

They followed their leader. Tad cycled the rear of the group. He smiled, noticing Billy's girth exceed the bike seat. He was an ass at times, but along with Jake, his best friend.

Jake turned left. "Don't go down there!" Billy shouted. "The bar will be closing this time of night. My Dad will be stumbling out!"

"Which way do you want to go?" he shouted.

"Go along Luna Park!" Tad shouted from the back. The whirring tyres against the sidewalk required a raise in voice. Luna Park was residential, probably as desolate as the area they found themselves now, and their best chance of staying undetected.

"Are you out of your mind?" Billy replied. "That leads on to Glenn!"

"Yeah, but not as far up as where the police are, dumbass!"

Jake swerved out ahead and on to the road, passing beneath a streetlight. Billy and Tad followed. They turned on to Luna Park.

Thunder bellowed across the sky. Tad ducked. "Shit!"

Billy crashed in to the back of Jake. "What did you stop for, idiot?"

"What the hell was that?"

Tad looked to the sky. "Hey, guys! Look at that!"

He pointed toward a star that shimmered within the nocturnal darkness. Its bright aura flickered. The light expanded continuously, gliding from across the horizon.

"An airplane?" Billy enquired.

"No way," Jake replied. "There's no noise."

Tad watched as the light approached. "A comet, or something? It has to be."

All three sat upon their saddles, staring to the star as it drew bigger and bigger from the heavens.

Tad quivered as a shiver passed through his spine. "It's getting closer." Its edges ruffled, flickering like flames. Trails of vapour swirled in its wake, hanging heavy where the comet passed. Gusts of wind rushed along the road. Tad's hair tickled, swaying in the invisible element. Billy's hood flapped, removing itself from his head. Debris swirled within the hidden vortex. The road trembled as the light tracked vertically above the houses, illuminating the entire street as it passed by.

"Awesome!" Tad shouted as the flames roared above Luna Park.

"Wow!" Billy sighed as they watched it pass out of town and toward the countryside. "Come on!"

"Come on, where?" Jake asked.

"Let's go see what it is!"

"I don't know if that's a good idea."

Billy growled. "Dammit, Jake! Look! It's coming down! Let's go be the first to discover it! We'll be famous!"

Adrenalin burst in to Tad's body. As a Sci-Fi fan his whole life, this was the moment he'd been awaiting. "Yeah! Come on! Chasing comets are worth getting in to trouble for!" Tad and Billy exploded from their position, standing upright on their pedals to gain more speed.

Tad looked behind as Jake peddled, shouting in their direction. "Hey! Hey! Wait up!"

Dogs barked from their yards. Sirens pierced the silence in the distance as the three raced along the street.

"I ain't never seen anything like that! Never!" Billy screamed from the front.

"Look! It's coming down close!" Tad shouted, his excitement too strong to contain. The light descended, quicker than he anticipated.

They swerved to the left, across the road and on to Glenn Avenue. Tad's excitement pulsed inside every nerve. His heart thudded, from adrenalin more than assertion. Across the horizon and amber hue swirled in to the sky. It expanded, illuminating the clouds that swirled in mass.

"Hey! Look!" Jake cried. "It's the same thing as last night!"

Tad looked to the sky once more, concentrating less on the empty road. It burned orange, illuminating their path as clear as the previous daylight would have done so.

"This is insane!" Tad laughed, feeling alive. Never had he been so excited.

They passed another junction and in to the small residential area. There was no police presence. Empty houses plastered with 'Police Line Do Not Cross' appeared in the night light.

"Yeehaw!" Billy screamed as they thundered past and out on to the country road.

In the distance the comet fell, crashing down in to the woodland that surrounded Shadow Oak Farm. Across the barking, across the sirens, the forest shattered in the distance.

"Holy shit! It's down!" Billy shouted.

"Not far!" Tad bellowed, pushing himself faster.

They cycled along the isolated road, bathed within the warm, summer light. Above the canopy a dome of white light pulsed, engulfing the trees. The dirt track leading to Shadow Oak appeared on their right. Billy turned, speeding so fast his rear wheel slid out across the debris. Away in the distance, a siren wailed.

Jake looked across his shoulder. "The cops!"

"Don't worry! We'll be heroes!" Billy replied.

They passed in to the trees until the greenery broke, cycling deeper and deeper in to the pine. A short distance away, light streamed en mass through the branches of the area, shadowing the trunks and bathing the forest.

Tad came to rest, dropping his bike without consideration. Billy and Jake followed suit, their cycles clattering down with little care or attention. The summer sky faded, receding back across the horizon to reveal patchy clouds and a cluster of stars. Tad hardly noticed. Staring at the aura, he moved in to the vegetation.

"What the hell is it?" Jake asked. "Aliens?"

"Maybe," Tad whispered before moving closer. He leant against a trunk.

Jake dropped to a squat, as if expecting a search light to shine across the area. "What are you doing?"

Tad turned back. "You want to find out what this thing is or not?"

The siren approached.

Billy grabbed his bike and threw it inside a patch of ferns. "I'll hide the bike-"

A reverberation pulsed through the ground. Jake leapt from his crouch and stood beside Tad. Tad reached down in to the darkness, placing his palm on the damp bracken. The pulse surged, thumping like a heartbeat within the earth itself. It distorted his senses, squeezing with force the inside of his head. An overwhelming fear washed throughout him. He dropped to the ground.

"Get down!" The aura crackled. Lightning snapped in forks between the tree trunks. A pulsing, electrical voltage snapped within the air. The aura burned so bright that Tad placed an arm across his eyes. "It's gonna blow!"

The ground trembled. Blasts of air powered between the trees. An explosion so loud, so deafening, rocked the entire woodland. Tad's eyes tightened. Light crept in at the edges. Jake fell against him. "Keep your eyes closed!" he shouted, not knowing if the others would hear. For a moment Tad recalled an airplane hitting turbulence. Everything about them swayed with violence. Leaves rustled. Branches creaked. Billy whined.

The wind stopped. The ground settled. Tad lay prone in the dirt, unsure how he managed to bury his face. Snapping voltage drew his attention. Staying down, he gathered his mind a moment longer.

"Guys. You okay?" Tad recognised Billy's voice, tainted with relief.

Jake sighed from somewhere. "Just about."

Tad peered upward. Lightning jumped between trunks and branches, reminding him of the Tesla machine in Fraknenstein's laboratory. The trees had been reduced to nothing more than charred bark, some expelling smoke. Its pungency overwhelmed the pine. Fire ravaged the rest, burning all with its amber beauty.

Fear overwhelmed Tad as a thought crossed his mind. He jumped up. "We gotta get out of here!" he snapped, jogging across to his bicycle. "If we get caught, we'll get blamed for it."

Along the track, red and blue lights flashed. He turned to see a squad car approach.

# Millers County Beat Officers 2354

Michael sat in shotgun, sipping the top of a hot coffee. He and Alex had been given beat, the only two officers on hand to show a presence inside The Fall. On a Friday, McGinty's Bar usually made the bulk of their calls.

"Can't believe how quiet it is?" Alex began. "We didn't put out a curfew or anything, did we?"

Michael shook his head. "Nah."

The Fall had been talking since the sky illuminated of its own accord the previous night. There had been talk of an eclipse, which most people brought in to, but a select few still chose to blame Mitchum Hoyt and his family.

He reached across to the radio. "This is car twelve to dispatch."

"This is dispatch, go ahead," Kim's voice crackled.

"Kim, this may sound a bit odd, but is everything okay? It's, what, five to midnight, and we haven't had anything come through yet. I know it's quiet here in Millers Fall, but this quiet on a Friday night?"

"We do get them, on the odd occasion."

"I know, but, like this?"

Kim released a partial laugh. "Seriously, Michael, we've had nothing, for any of the services. Everyone seems to be within a state of well-being, people are turning off their cookers and extinguishing cigarettes in the correct manner, and also behaving well under the influence of alcohol."

"We took station outside McGinty's, and have seen about three people come and go so far. It feels like we're patrolling a graveyard."

"You two should make the most of it. Tomorrow is a different day. Things might pick up for you then, but in the meantime just patrol, show the public you're out and about. That can be just important."

Alex brought the car to life.

"Will do. We're heading out now, anyways."

"Stay safe. We *will* let you know if anything happens."

Michael replaced the handset as Alex pulled in to the road. "Something's not right."

Alex flashed a glance to him. "What do you mean?"

"I don't know, I just got that feeling, you know? We've been working together over five years, and I ain't never known it this quiet, not ever. It feels like you could cut the atmosphere out there."

Alex ducked, checking the road signals as they drove by. "It must be the eclipse. I think it scared a lot of people. If I was a betting man I'd place money that everyone is at home, and probably waiting for it to happen again."

They passed out to the western boarder of town where vast openness led seventy miles to Port Sandown.

"Pull over a minute."

"What's wrong?"

"Just pull over. I gotta take a leek."

Alex pulled on to a small track beside a coppice. The interior lights stunned Michael as he opened the door.

"Don't get seen. This is the sort of thing we get suspended for."

"Yeah, yeah, yeah." He slammed the door and wandered in to the vegetation, brushing against leaves until hidden from the road. A bush, at shoulder height, concealed his modesty whilst still allowing him the pleasurable view of a countryside bathed in starlight. Adjusting his zipper, Michael looked up, noticing a star. He continued to watch whilst splashing the greenery. The star was bright, and approaching. "No way," he said, listening to the expelled water rattling the leaves. But it was. The star was coming down. And fast. Within a few seconds it was clear the object was not a star. "Crap!" he dashed through the coppice, fumbling with his zipper.

"Alex!"

"Got it," Alex responded.

Michael dove on to the passenger seat. "What the hell is it?" he asked, slamming the door.

"A comet. Looks like It's about to crash."

Alex spun the car, throwing him against the window.

"Car twelve, this is dispatch."

Michael snatched the radio. "Go ahead, dispatch."

"We've got reports of a large light in the sky-"

"On it, Kim. Looks like a comet. We're chasing it now."

"Chasing it?"

"It's losing trajectory. Get fire and EMT on standby." Alex brought the siren to life. "We're following."

Michael looked to the light. "That thing's close."

"It's fast, too," Alex responded. "I'm pushing one hundred. It might clear us travelling at that speed."

"My God!"

"What?"

"Look!"

Alex followed Michael's instruction. A warm, amber sky emerged from the midnight darkness. Shadows cast across the speeding ground. "The eclipse? Again?"

"This is unbelievable!"

"Dispatch, we got the same thing as last night out here too. Goddamn orange sky."

"Christ. What the hell is it?" Kim responded.

"No idea."

The patrol car thundered through Millers Fall. The siren wailed through the emptiness. Within the sky their target drifted to the left.

"Make a left here," Michael ordered.

Alex threw the car around the empty junction. The light appeared to their right, trailed by a vapour line that swirled grey against the orange clouds.

"I told you!" Michael shouted. "I told you something was wrong!"

"Car twelve, status update."

His attention returned to the radio. "We're heading north along Finsbury Boulevard. The light, comet, meteor, whatever, is travelling at a hell of a speed. Looks like it may fall in the open, away from the populated areas."

"Finger's crossed."

Michael left his seat as Alex ignored the road. The odd bystander stood, gaping at the light, the sky, and now the patrol car in pursuit. Their wheels screamed as they took the next corner, heading east. His view became distorted. "For sure. It's definitely coming down."

"I've got visual," Alex stated.

"Keep going."

"Damn." Alex shook his head. The shadows from surrounding buildings stretched across the road.

Michael rubbed a hand across his chin. "This is sure-to-hell no eclipse. Eclipse's take the light away, not make it brighter."

"How's the direction?"

"Still veering left." They approached the next junction. Alex doglegged left then right, on to Luna Park. Michael held observation. "Down! Down! I've lost it beyond the houses!"

"I'm heading out on Glenn."

The car reached the junction with Glenn Avenue and turned, thundering past the last line of empty homes.

"God damn! Look at that!" Michael pointed out to the woodland up ahead. It bathed in a wondrous, white aura, broken by the pulsing, amber glow of flames.

"Shit! Fire! Call it in!" Alex ordered.

"Dispatch, this is car twelve! Kim, we need the fire department out here right now! On the turning to Shadow Oak Farm! The damn woods is on fire!"

"Roger, dispatching now." Kim could not hide concern, even over a radio.

Michael dropped the radio, glaring at the fire as they approached. "Look at it!"

Alex looked around. "Michael."

He peered through the windscreen as they thundered across the road. The sky faded. The sunset diminished, as it had done the previous night. As quickly as it had risen, the orange sky returned to its natural, darkened state. Alex threw the patrol car on to the farm track. He pointed ahead. "Up there! Look!"

Michael looked on, finding three boys stood beside the track about to make a getaway. "I don't believe it!" he said, opening the door as they bore down upon them.

The patrol car skidded beside the trio of boys. He jumped out, greeted by the pulsing heat and roaring flames devouring the trees.

# The Woodland 2354

Cane studied his map with the flashlight. The day plotting the co-ordinates had been a strain, and still didn't guarantee any success. The division had traced the anomaly since it entered our cluster some six months ago, causing apprehension and maybe just a bit of excitement. The division leader, Agent Lynch, had more than a passing interest in this event. It was difficult to comprehend, even to himself and other senior division operatives, but whatever it was, it was big.

Placing the compass on the paper he orientated himself to the west. If the calculations were correct, this is the line it would follow on declined. The point of impact was a few hundred metres or so away. Risky, but given what was at stake, worth it.

Turning the flashlight off, Cane rolled his head back, closed his eyes and exhaled. It was beginning to get chilly. Stars appeared between branches as his eyes opened. One in particular, appeared brighter. A flutter of adrenalin swirled within his stomach. The cell phone raised to his ear as quickly as his eyes had opened.

"It's me. I have visual."

"The location you submitted. Is it correct?"

Cane frowned, unable to place the voice. "Affirmative." The star twinkled as it rushed toward him. "Within the vicinity for certain."

The line crackled. The earpiece hissed and blipped as the broken voice attempted to push through.

"Division. You're breaking up…."

Cane ended the call, not prepared to fight with his device. The voice of caution began whispering in his subconscious. He traversed the terrain to allow more space between himself and the impact zone.

Through the silence the light roared. Smoke followed, leaving its own sky trail in the cold air. Was this how an angel fell? Was this a replication of Lucifer's fall from the heavens?

The sky groaned. The light roared. Canopies broke. This was an aircraft crash. Cane fell as the impact coursed through the ground. Light engulfed the woodland. Fire began in an instant. He sat up, fumbling for the torch that fell beside him as the aura faded. Finding it, he switched it on and sprinted toward the flames. Snagging on a branch, he dropped his rucksack and rushed forward, approaching the amber hue and isolated flames catching exposed branches. Good job he moved, or he'd have been caught within the area.

Cane found himself near to a track. He scoured the area, searching for a sign of life. *'There's no way anyone could survive that. No way.'*

A scream bellowed from the flames. The tortured, piercing wail pushed gooseflesh across Cane's skin. A palm emerged from the fire. Flames feasted on the little flesh remaining. A skull appeared, its jaw hung limp as blood and liquid oozed from every orifice. The body stuttered and stumbled as it cooked within the trees. Cane stepped back, his mind lost with fear. The melting body beckoned, reached to him, before vanishing behind an amber wall. Its cries ceased.

Cane returned to reality as the sound of voices approached. Not far away a siren wailed. The place would be crawling in next to no time. Blocked by the voices, Cane turned and sprinted back in to the tree's where he had approached from, hoping that his presence remained unnoticed.

# 8

"Get back!" Michael yelled, sprinting across to the kids. Each appeared lost, unable to think for themselves. He grimaced. "Tad? What the hell are you doing out here?"

Tad mumbled. "It wasn't us! We followed it! It crashed here!"

He placed a hand on the boy's shoulder. "Get back. You all alright?"

"We're fine," Billy replied, as both he and Jake followed.

"It's true, officer. We just followed it from the sky," Jake added, confirming the story.

"Alright, alright. Is there anyone else with you?"

"No," Tad replied, "just us."

Michael nodded. Their eyes met, and through whatever reason, a hunch maybe, he knew Tad wasn't lying. "Alex!" he shouted across the open.

Alex looked up. He was leaning against the car door, speaking to dispatch. Michael pointed to the three boys, then across the track. Alex nodded. "Over here," Alex ordered, gesturing with his free hand.

Michael encouraged Tad with a firm push and turned to the fire. Through the flames and haze appeared a group of people. "The hell?" he whispered, in disbelief.

"You three head out to the road and direct the fire truck this way," Alex ordered as the boys reached him.

"There's people in there!" Michael shouted.

"You're kidding?" Alex replied.

Michael raced in to the woodland, shielding his face from the heat. About him the trees burned, surrounding him in some kind of Hell, one he imagined the Devil to preside within. The flames we're so hot, maybe he'd make an appearance in these woods.

Through the blaze a group of people emerged. Their leader, first in line, threw buckets of water in to the carnage.

"Get back!" Michael shouted. "Get back!"

The leader looked to him. With panic etched across his face, Mitchum Hoyt returned the gaze. "Help us! Help us!" he pleaded.

The pungent aroma of burning bark filled the air. Michael coughed, still shielding away from the heat. Smoke poked at his eyes. "Get back! The fire department is coming!" He waved his hand away. Mitchum took notice. Sirens wailed above the chaos. "Get back!"

Hoyt looked to his people, then back to Michael, nodding in agreement. Placing his arms out, he pushed the bearded clan of followers back in to the darkness.

Michael turned back. "Goddamn freaks," he whispered. A hand grasped his shoulder, dragging him from the inferno. With eyes closed he bundled across the terrain, coughing as the fresh, cold air struck him. Leaning over he hocked, spitting the taste of burning woodland from his mouth.

"You could have gotten yourself killed!" Alex snapped.

Michael nodded. "Maybe." He spluttered once more. "But Hoyt wouldn't have left without my say so."

The fire truck groaned as it approached. Alex pushed him from its path. The siren died. Hearing doors open, Michael opened his eyes as firefighters emerged, one after the other.

"Anyone in there?" one asked, rallying his men.

"There was, but they retreated," he replied, drawing a deep breath before coughing once more.

"Which way?"

"In to the woods."

The firefighters donned their equipment and opened the truck, revealing hoses and various firefighting equipment.

Alex patted Michael. "Next time we have a quiet shift, just keep your damn mouth shut."

***

Sheriff Palmer finished his conversation with the fire department and headed to the cluster of patrol cars gathered on the track. The fire had been controlled quicker than he expected, a testament to those of the department. This had reduced the damage to the surrounding area. As far as he could tell, at least, Mitchum Hoyt's farm had remained untouched.

"They're gonna remain here," he began, approaching his staff. Agent's Davis and Welsh were on hand, having hitched a ride across in the Sheriff's vehicle. "They want to make sure it doesn't flare up. Did you get the boys statements?"

Alex nodded. "Yeah. Parents have been to pick them up, too."

"You think they had anything to do with it?"

Michael shook his head. "No, we saw the same thing they did."

Palmer looked across his shoulder. The trees illuminated with the artificial light emanating from the fire truck. "Problem is, there's nothing there."

"You have to be kidding me?" Alex replied.

"No. I'm one hundred percent telling you, there's no debris or anything in that location."

Agent Davis drew on a cigarette, his lips popping as it removed. "Bullshit, Sheriff. We saw it. Everyone saw it. That comet came down right here, and your telling me there's no evidence it landed?"

"That's exactly what I'm telling you." Davis looked to Welsh, who shrugged.

Davis exhaled and threw the butt on to the track. "When this is clear, get your men out." He waved a finger to the woodland. "I want to find out exactly what the hell is happening, starting here."

Palmer gave a telling glare to Alex. "Alright, you two, back to the station, write up the report. What were the kids doing out this late, anyway?"

"Long story. They we're heading somewhere else, but saw the comet and chased it down, much like we did."

Palmer nodded. "Get back and write it up. I'll catch up with you both later."

Michael and Alex jumped in their vehicle. Palmer moved to his own, gesturing for the agents to do the same.

"I'll admit, I've been to some strange places in my time," Davis began, slumping in shotgun beside Palmer, "but this place? Millers Fall? Sunset at midnight? Comets with no substance? Your currently top of my list, Sheriff."

***

From the safety of the woodland opposite the fire, Cane sat silent, concealed by the darkness. The body he'd seen was a vessel, an indiscreet way to hide a life-form that could be destroyed on impact. That was what had happened. There was no evidence to be found because it had been burned up at such an intense heat nothing was left.

Two things came from this jaunt in to the woodlands. Number one, he now knew where Mitchum Hoyt was to be found, and second, another life form had made contact.

# 9

Palmer cruised within the speed limit. Small talk with the Bureau's finest had been exhausted. He came to a standstill underneath a set of lights. The shops, empty for the night, slumbered in the townsfolk absence. No-one wandered the sidewalks. No headlights passed, and hadn't done on his entire journey.

The light turned green. Palmer pulled away, checking right for oncoming traffic.

"Look out!"

The brake stomped to the floor, jolting the car forward. A bloodied hand planted the hood as a body smashed in to the vehicles grate and fell to the road.

"Shit!" Davis cried, throwing his door open.

Palmer launched from the wheel. "I wasn't travelling that fast!"

Davis reached the bonnet, drawing his gun. "Stay down! Stay, the hell, down!" Welsh appeared beside him.

Palmer pulled his Glock and aimed down at the naked man cowering on the tarmac. "My God…"

The man lurched upright, shielding his eyes with open palms. His skin, from head to toe, saturated in blood.

"Hands up! Get your hands up!" Davis boomed.

He trembled and cowered, raising the palms as requested. Palmer noted the mumblings of Agent Welsh on the car radio.

"Cuff him!" Davis ordered.

Palmer lowered the handgun and reached for his cuffs. Trying not to make contact with the blood, they snapped in place around his wrists.

The man glared back to the Sheriff with wide, fearful eyes.

Palmer gasped. "Finn? Finn, is that you?"

"You know him?" Davis snapped.

"Jesus Christ, Finn, what have you done?

*** 

Officer Andy Loveridge flanked Sergeant Harris as they power marched through the corridor. The department was so short of bodies that even the big cheese was called back to the beat.

Their footfalls merged upon the shining surface as they burst through a set of double doors. By the nurses' station up ahead, the Sheriff and Agents loitered.

"Is it him?" Harris asked as they joined their seniors.

Palmer nodded, but something was wrong. His expression was one of sorrow. "Yeah, it's him."

"What's wrong?" Andy asked, seizing the opportunity.

The Sheriff looked back. "You both packing?"

"Of course," Harris replied.

"They're doing tests. We found him in the middle of town. Idiot ran out in front of the car." Palmer sighed. "He ain't right. They had to sedate him to run the tests and check him over. That ain't the worst of it. He was covered from head to toe in blood."

"Shit. How hard did you hit him?" Harris asked.

"Not that hard. I was pulling away at the lights. Made contact at no more than twenty miles an hour."

Andy began to probe a little. "So, if you didn't cause his injuries...."

"We don't know who did. But the amount he was showered in, I don't think it was his."

Andy's jaw hung agape. "No way?"

"Afraid so. It kills me to do this, but we need his room guarded round the clock." Palmer dropped his voice. "We may be dealing with a killer."

"Shit," Andy sighed, dismayed that a colleague and friend could do such a thing.

"We're not one hundred percent certain, not yet at least, but we will be questioning him as soon as he's able."

The door to Finn's room opened, and a doctor of Japanese origin exited.

"Doctor, you tell us anything?" Agent Davis asked.

The doctor made his way across to the vacant station and dropped some papers on the desk. "We won't know anything for certain until the results are in, but judging by his examination, he appears fine. There's a little bruising around his right hip, where he made contact with the car, but I can't find any other sign of injury."

"What about the blood?" the Sheriff enquired.

"They're cleaning him up now."

"No, I mean, was it his?"

The doctor pulled a pen from his pocket and began scribbling on some document. "I just took samples which I'll get to the lab now. They're labelled emergency, which means the results should be in fairly quick."

"How quick is fairly quick?" Davis asked.

"An hour. Two at most."

He sighed. "Sheesh."

"Andy." Andy shifted his gaze from the Agent to the Sheriff. "I want you to take watch here for the remainder of the shift."

"Sure."

The doctor looked to Davis. "I can have the results given to the police officer standing guard, if you are not here when they come in."

Davis nodded. "Fine. But is he ready for questioning now?"

"His anxiety appears to be lowering. Physically, I'd say yes. He's cognitive and settled, the sedation appears to have worked. I'm not a psychiatrist, though. I have no idea if he could cope, simply because we don't know what he's gone through." The doctor signed his paperwork and left it at the seat of the station. "The nurses will be out any minute. They both know you may want to see him. If you want to try talking, you can do so then."

"Thank you."

The doctor nodded as he left the station. Somewhere in his jacket, his pager bleeped.

"Andy and I will go in," the Sheriff stated. "We're both familiar to him. If what the doctor says is right, I don't want to overload him."

Davis glared for a moment, then walked to Palmer with a swagger.

"We're in charge here, Sheriff, not you. We'll make the decisions, got it?"

Palmer spoke firm. "Maybe. But Millers Fall is my town. These are my officers. And this may be our one chance at knowing what happened to my men and those families up on Glenn Avenue. You heard the doctor. We could send him in to some kind of mental lapse if this is not done right. You want to report to your superiors that you broke our key witness in this case?"

Davis turned, looking to Welsh. Welsh responded with his usual, silent shrug.

"Alright, but you listen to me." He pointed at Palmer. "You screw this up and I'll make sure you're your only fit to flip burgers. You got that?"

"Would you like Sergeant Harris to run you back in to Millers Fall?"

"Nah, we'll find our own way." Davis barged past the officers, followed by the calculating Welsh. "As soon as those results are in, call me."

The Sheriff tipped his hat. "Will do, sir."

The Agents vanished behind the doors. Andy sighed. "Phew. That guy is one, serious, asshole."

Harris placed a hand on his shoulder. "It's the other one you have to watch out for, studying us all behind those glasses of his. I bet he's the one running the show."

"Either way, just forget it for now," the Sheriff replied, removing his Stetson. "We got more important things to worry about."

Two nurses left Finn's room. "He should be ok if you want to see him," one stated, making her way around the station desk.

Palmer smiled as they passed. "Sergeant, find a seat to be stationed at the door, please. Andy?"

The Sheriff gestured his head toward the gloomy room. Andy acknowledged and entered first, stepping across the threshold and in to an investigation.

Finn laid beneath the sheets, his upper body inclined and hidden beneath the standard issue gown. He bore a little more than the 5 o'clock shadow he'd grown since the last time they'd met. His Adam's apple bobbled. Finn turned toward them, rolling his head within the pillows.

"Andy." Andy smiled and pulled up a chair. "Sheriff? You too?"

"Me too, Finn. How you holding up?"

Finn smiled. "I've been better," he replied, his voice just audible. To Andy, his voice gave a report of dehydration, as if he'd been lost in a desert instead of The Fall.

"We contacted your family. They're heading here now. Should be with you by dawn." Finn nodded. "Are you, you know, feeling up to-"

"I'm a police officer, Sheriff. You want to ask me some questions, right?"

"That's what I'd like."

"Only if you feel up to it," Andy said, noting the discontent in Finn's voice.

"It's fine."

Palmer placed his hat on the table and perched at the foot of the bed. "You sure? We can come back later. It's just, I'd rather you speak to me than the Feds, that's all."

"The Feds?"

"When five, armed police officers vanish in to thin air, along with the population of the area they're operating in, there's gonna be a hell of a lot of attention drawn, and from all the senior organisations our great country provides."

"Have you found them? The families? The others? Tina? Oscar? Benny? Max?"

Palmer shook his head. "No. You're the first. Just over a day you've been gone, until you decided to throw yourself in front of my car."

"Really?"

"Yep. Good job I was just pulling away, otherwise you'd be laying here with more than just a few bruises."

Finn sighed. "I'm sorry, sir. First thing I remember is the emergency room."

Andy leaned closer. "What about before? You remember where you were, or how the hell you got there?"

Finn closed his eyes. After a moment of silence, his lower lip trembled. A tear shed down on to the pillow.

"Hey? Are you okay?" Palmer asked, leaning in.

"Yeah," Finn snivelled, wiping the tears from his face. "Yeah, but I only remember a bit. I don't know what happened to me. One minute we were there, the next, I was under the glare of the lights with doctors rushing about the place. Between the two, I remember sorrow. I remember being so scared and frightened for the others. I remember crying. And I remember the cries coming from the light."

"What light?" Palmer enquired.

"I think we were in some kind of room. I remember hearing the rest just wailing, completely, just, in pure pain and terror. Tina's cries, they cut right through me. I've never heard anything so horrendous in my life, not a damn thing."

"You remember what was happening in there?"

Finn shook his head and wiped mucus away with a tissue that had been placed at the bedside.

"No, but whatever it was, it was evil. I sensed it. I remember seeing a shadow. A person. They looked like priests. Black gowns stood against the light. That's it. That's all I can recall."

"Okay, Finn." Palmer smiled, patting his thigh. "Get some rest. Andy's gonna sit outside, making sure you don't get disturbed unless it's needed."

Andy rose from his seat. He was shocked at how his friend appeared, sobbing like a child. Something troubled Finn, he knew it.

"I'll be just there. You need anything, yell."

Finn nodded, wiping tears with another tissue.

Palmer placed his hat on. "Rest up, Finn. I'll call by tomorrow, see how you're doing."

"Thanks."

\*\*\*

The three officers converged outside the room, beside the nurse's station. The Sheriff relayed everything back to Sergeant Harris.

"Something's not right. To just burst in to tears like that," Palmer mused. Andy saw the look of discontent upon his face.

"You believe him?" Harris asked.

"I don't know. He never made mention of the blood we found him swamped in, which I expected him to explain first. He's troubled, for sure. Something's scared him, whether it's his own actions or those of another, I don't know. Anyway, we're not getting any more, at least for the time being. Andy, when the results arrive, call me. I'll send someone to take over when you finish."

Andy nodded. "Gotcha. I'll keep an eye on him."

\*\*\*

Later that night, as Palmer slumped in to bed, his cell rang, illuminating the bedroom. Officer Loveridge was attempting to gain contact.

"Andy? The test results in?"

"Yes, sir, they are."

Andy's voice was anxious. He sat upright. "Hey? What is it? What's wrong?"

"Sir, you're not going to believe it."

"What?"

"I think you'll want to see this for yourself."

# 10

"Explain to me now, why, at three o'clock in the Goddamn morning, I have to lecture you both about acting your God-damned age? We're you two born this dumb or did you just get good at it?"

Tad and Sam sat in their lounge. The very fact they were together was a sign they'd done something wrong. Tad hated Sam with a passion, and the feeling was more than mutual. Being the youngest, Tad often felt the brunt of his brother's rage. It also didn't help that he'd been adopted as an infant. His parents had been honest right the way through childhood, informing him he was in fact taken in, and hadn't tried to hide it in any way. Tad believed his adoption was the reason Sam acted the way he did. Sometimes, He could empathise with Sam, being an only child and bathed in the affections of both parents. Then, a kid shows up in your home, a kid cut from a different cloth with no blood to bond, and the dynamic was surely going to change. The more Tad thought, the more he accepted, until one day he realised Sam would never, or could never, be a brother to him. No way on this earth. From that day forward, Tad gave up trying. Sam was clever as a bully, though. He was sly, able to cover up his misdoings. He ruled Tad like a dictator, threatening beatings and other acts of violence if he spoke out. At this precise time, Tad was very much afraid. Not from his adopted parents, but Sam. He would retaliate for this, of which there was no doubt.

After coming clean to the police about why he and the others were out so late, the police visited the trash behind the store to find Lance, Sam's best friend, wearing a hockey mask and waiting to scare the crap out of them. Childish? Of course. Tad was more embarrassed that he'd fallen for it. Jake would be in for hell when he got home. Billy? Well, he would be if his Dad was there. If he was lucky, it was only his Mom, and she'd cover for him. Now, though, he sat beside the guy who masterminded the whole scenario, feeling the wrath of their father.

"Dave, that's enough," their mother interrupted.

Dave turned away, placing a hand on his hips. "Get upstairs, the both of you." Tad stood in unison with Sam and left the lounge without uttering a word. "One more thing," their Dad shouted, drawing their attention. "You're both grounded. For a week."

"Oh come on!" Sam snapped. Tad dropped his head and climbed the stairs.

"Don't argue with me, Sam."

"But I'm going out with-"

"I don't care what the hell you were doing, you're not anymore! You want to act like a child? I'll treat you like one. It's things like this that will get a scholarship withdrawn, you understand that? And you're supposed to be starting one this year! Get out of my sight, before I make it two weeks."

Tad closed his bedroom door as Sam approached, muttering some profanity about his punishment.

***

Tad kicked his clothes across the room and drew back his duvet. It had been a long night, which only hit him as he got ready for bed. The door flew open. Sam bounded across the room and punched him through the duvet.

"You little bastard!" After the repeated punches, a slap jerked Tad's head sideways. "This is just the beginning. You wanna mess with my life? I'll sure as hell mess with yours. Sleep tight, asshole!" Sam pushed Tad in to the mattress then left the room.

"What the hell are you two doing up there now?"

Sam looked back. "Nothing, Dad. Just grabbing a DVD from Tad's room." He smirked, flipping Tad the bird.

"Get back in your own damn room!"

"Sure, Dad. Sorry." He pointed back at Tad. "You're dead, you punk ass little piece of crap. I'm gonna beat you so damned hard, Mom and Dad won't recognise you."

Sam glared one final time before disappearing back to his own room. Tad curled the duvet around him, his ribs and torso aching from the strikes inflicted by his step-brother. Tears flooded, but he remained silent, unwilling to draw any attention.

He lay there, crying until he fell asleep.

## 11

Palmer sat behind his desk. It was still dark, but he knew dawn would break soon. It was pointless going back home after this, for, what? Three hours sleep? He may as well just stay at the station, overload on caffeine and let the Agent's run the show. Harris sat to his side, arms folded. He looked troubled.

"I don't believe it. Of all the people."

Palmer echoed Harris' sentiment. Agent Davis approached the office. "Here we go," Palmer replied, drawing the Sergeant's attention to the open door.

"Hit me with it." Davis strolled inside, his cream jacket flapping un-buttoned about him.

Palmer gestured to the empty chair. "Results came back on the blood we found on him."

"What did it conclude?"

"It concluded what we initially thought. The blood was not his own."

"Do they know who it belongs to?"

The Sheriff rubbed his forehead. "Partly."

"Partly? What the hell do you mean 'partly?'"

Palmer threw the report across his desk. "It means that they only traced the blood on him to people they had on record. From the sample they took were fourteen different blood types. Eleven of them could be identified. All of the police officers who went missing with him, and some of the family members who vanished along with them."

Davis scoured the report. "You've got to be kidding me?"

"No. No, we're not. The facts don't lie."

Palmer watched as Davis read every single word in the report, his eyes darting back and forth along the lines. "He'll go to the chair."

"Let's not jump to conclusions," the Sheriff began, irked by Davis' attitude. "There's something not right here."

"You're damn right about that. A police officer killing fourteen people is more than 'not right.' He's a disgrace...."

"Now that's enough!" Palmer slammed a hand on his desk. "You people waltz in to my department, take control of my staff and judge everyone without considering the facts! I'm telling you to do some old fashioned, god damned police work! I've known Officer Renton since he was a kid. I've seen him grow up and transition in to a damn fine police officer. For him to do something like this is way out of character. I can't imagine it for a second. I'm going to investigate the case, leaving no stone unturned. If we gather overwhelming evidence against him, I will take to the stands and testify against him myself, but until then, I'm going to find out exactly what happened. You don't like it? Run your ass back home to Mommy, tell them what I'm doing and get me suspended. You got it?"

Palmer didn't know what response he'd receive, but this damn Agent Davis had finally worn him through.

Davis threw the papers back on the desk, leant back in the chair and crossed his legs. "Alright, we'll do it your way." His demeanour was calm, as was his tone. "You're absolutely right. If Officer Renton is innocent, pursuing a case against him is the last thing I want. The evidence is pointing directly toward him, though. You don't get smeared in fourteen different blood samples without being involved in some kind of misdemeanour. You conduct a thorough investigation. Agent Welsh, the Bureau and I will assist you however you need. But I warn you. Mess this up and your head will fall. You got that?"

"I got it."

Davis stood. "In that case, I'll bid you good night. Agent Welsh and I will be here at ten in the morning. We'll support you in anyway, but be warned. Legally, we're the ones running this little shindig, and I'm not accepting anything less than your best efforts. If I think for one second your interests are not impartial and to the letter of the law,

I'll pull you out and make damn sure you take my order in McDonalds before I leave this town. Do we have a deal?"

Palmer saw the intent in Davis' eyes. "We do." He remained terse.

"This is your show, Sheriff. The eyes are on you."

\*\*\*

Officer Michael York arrived home just before nine. The cloudless sky promised him a good day. Too bad he'd be back in work later. He pulled the car on to the drive and parked in front of the garage door. Across the white picket fence, his neighbour's kid was prepping a lawn mower ready to cut the grass.

"Hey, I hope you're going to be done by ten. I'm gonna be sleeping from then." Tad looked up and smiled half-heartedly. It looked like he'd been told off, grounded or both. "Is this your punishment?"

Tad nodded. "Yup. Part of, at least. I got grounded for a week, too."

Michael smiled. "You know, if I'd have been one of you guys, I'd have done the exact same thing. Town's buzzing about the meteor this morning. Everywhere I've been, they're all asking me about it." Tad appeared troubled. Something was weighing him down. Michael approached the fence. "You okay?"

"Yeah. Yeah, I'm good. But there's one thing I don't understand. Where was the meteor? All we found up there was fire. No rocks, no stones, no nothing."

Even though off duty, Michael was still bound by data protection. "I don't know. I'm guessing it burned up in the atmosphere or something?"

Tad shook his head. "No. No way. I'm a science and sci-fi geek. There's no way a meteor that size would burn out before impact. It'd be impossible. You saw the size of it?"

"Yes, I did." Come to think of it, the kid had a point, but maybe not one worth dwelling on now. "Listen, I wouldn't worry too much about it. There's nothing left up there. We searched the forest with the fire department. Apart from some burnt trees, there's nothing interesting."

Tad smiled, only this time it was genuine. "You'd say that anyway, Officer York."

Michael winked and began the walk to his front door. "Take it easy, buddy. And if you wake me up with that thing, I'll haul your ass in for anti-social behaviour."

# 12

Sam was grounded, but it didn't stop him researching his next project. The fact was, if it was a week day and it was Mom at home, he'd flip her the bird and go do whatever he wanted. It wasn't to be, however. Dad was in, and he'd beat the holy hell out of Sam and his brother if they went against his wishes.

Sam recalled the rage and anger that festered within their father, and had done for many years. He was often the brunt of the rage. Tad was such a goody two-shoes, and Mom loved him that much more. Maybe it was years of being beaten by their Dad, while he was drunk or just pissed off, but Sam's release was beating on his younger brother. There wasn't even a small amount of regret, knowing Dad would swing his fists around freely. Tad pissed him off, and got what he deserved.

He leant back in the chair. The thing was, beating Tad just wasn't doing it any more. The satisfaction wasn't there. Tad's face appeared inside his mind. Sam clenched his fist. God, how much did he despise him?

The first part of the plan had worked. Tad had been gullible enough to believe him about the DVD's in the alley. Now the evidence was there that Tad was indeed a gullible, dumb-ass idiot. The second part had been completed some time ago. Sam's smile increased. He was clever, and knew it. Heading to the backwoods at Shadow Oak Farm was genius. The entire population of Millers Fall suspected those hillbillies of everything that went wrong in the town. Everything. Didn't matter what it was, if it was bad, they had something to do with it. Look at the two guys who went missing a few months ago. The Fall believed Hoyt and his people took them. It didn't matter if they didn't, they were the ones to be blamed. That would provide the perfect alibi.

Mom, he hated as much as Tad. To ruin her life would be a fine achievement. Dad, he didn't care much for either, but knew the old man could beat him down with little effort. The plan was coming together.

## 13

Diana wandered to the till of Denny's Groceries. Her working week was ever increasing, but she didn't mind. Nothing had captured The Fall quite like the sunset at midnight or the vanishing residents. It was a horrible event to befall such a small population, but nothing unites a community like a mystery. Everyone was concerned, not just for the wellbeing of themselves and their families, but for the missing people, too.

At the till, four women chatted to Denny. One, Nicky Hayden had in tow her five year old son, Noah. Sally Archer and Lorraine Cassidy were there also, The Fall's resident busybodies. Every town had them. The final lady, Natalie Clark, was an old school friend of Diana's.

Denny noticed as she headed across and smiled.

"Any word from the Police Department?" Sally asked.

Diana shook her head. "No. Nothing yet to report." She knew damn well there was, but breach of confidentiality was more than her job's worth. Plus, there was no way in hell she wanted these women to find out.

"What about the meteor?" Nicky asked. Noah tugged on her arm.

"That was pretty scary," Denny said as he rang through Diana's items. "Terrible thing that it struck the woodland out there, but it could have been much, much worse. Imagine what would have happened if it'd fallen in town?"

The bell to the door tinged as someone entered.

"Mommy, look."

"Wait a minute, Noah."

"I heard the FBI is in town?" Lorraine asked.

Diana played ignorant. "I've been in the dispatch room and on the beat all week. I have no idea."

"Mommy!"

"Noah! For Christ-"

"Good morning, to good people."

Diana turned. There, smiling beneath a scraggly beard, stood Mitchum Hoyt. He stood with both hands in his trouser pockets. An open shirt revealed a vest tightened against a rotund midriff. From beneath his straw Fedora, his long hair rested atop his shoulders. Mister McAllum and the woman clad in the old style dress joined him.

"We need to stop by and pick up a few supplies."

Denny stuttered. "Err, yes. Yes. By all means."

Hoyt tipped his head. "Much obliged. Mister McAllum, Miss Olivia, if you would, please?"

Hoyt's accomplices took hold of a basket each and entered the aisles. Everyone inside stopped, even the customers.

Hoyt paced. "Certainly had a strange few days around these parts, haven't we? What with orange skies at midnight and now stars falling from the heavens? Makes you wonder just what is going on. Everything okay here? In town, I mean."

Diana took it upon herself to answer. "As good as we can hope for."

"Ah, Officer Trent. A pleasure to meet you again." He wandered past Natalie. "Ma'am." The store fell silent, save for the sound of Mister McAllum and Miss Olivia taking items and wandering the aisles. "Any word on those missing boys yet?"

"No. They're still missing."

Hoyt shook his head. "Truly, truly dreadful. Especially to some so young. I wonder what the world is coming to these days. War, commercialism and crime run rife throughout all communities of our great country. It's the expectancy of how we should live and thus the rules from which you abide. Not me, though," he chuckled. "I march to the beat of my own drum. My friends and I allow that lifestyle to pass us by. We take pleasure in the simple things, such as a fine and beautiful day like today. When was the last time you stopped to admire such a thing? A bright, cloudless sky? The smell of pine on the breeze? Dew drops glistening by dawn's first light." He smiled. "Even the frost glistening on a winter's morn, as cold as it may be."

Hoyt wandered to the counter.

"My Daddy says you took the boys."

"Noah! Shut up!" Nicky snapped.

Hoyt looked down. A cherub-faced, red headed child with an expression of innocence looked back. "I admire your honesty, Noah." Nicky shot a glare to Diana. Diana gestured back with her expression, one that implied to remain calm.

Hoyt took a candy bar and squatted in front of the boy. "It takes a brave person to say what they feel, especially when it comes to matters such as this. I can bet you a dollar not one of the grownups here would say that to me, face to face, the same way you have, even though they agree with your Daddy. What do you think? Do you think I took those boys?"

Noah shook his head. "No."

"Well, thank you, Noah. Thank you very much for your support." Hoyt looked to Denny and raised the candy bar. "Add this to my bill, please. This is for you, young sir, for being so honest. I want you to remember one thing. No matter what happens to you, whether it be in school, in the playground or whatever situation you find yourself in, you must always, *always* tell the truth." Noah took the candy. Hoyt stood and ruffled his hair. Mister McAllum and Miss Olivia returned from the aisles. Diana and Natalie stepped back, allowing them access to the till. "A wonderful boy you have there, ma'am. Such a pleasure speaking with him. A true pleasure." Hoyt tipped his hat to Nicky. "Now, Officer Trent, you must keep me informed of any developments with the recent activity on my farm."

"I will, Mister Hoyt. How is your property after last night?"

"Thankfully untouched, the buildings at least. The patch that fell to the fire is still smouldering, but nothing now that we can't handle. I have every faith that the fire department served us to the utmost of its ability. In the meantime, we will keep a close observation on the area, just to be sure."

"It may be an idea to have a telephone, just in case you require emergency assistance in the future."

Hoyt threw his head back and laughed. "Officer Trent. For centuries, as a species, we existed without phones, television and electricity. What makes today any different? A simple life is a meaningful life. Rest assured that if we need assistance, we will reach you."

"Err, Mister Hoyt? That will be seventy two, seventy eight, please?"

Hoyt turned to Denny. Miss Olivia bagged their goods. Diana watched as matches, soap and various other items entered the brown, paper bag.

"It certainly will," Hoyt replied, moving to the counter. He pulled a roll of money from a pocket. "Here you are, my friend, and not a cent less. Whatever change I am due you may keep, for the gracious hospitality you and your customers have given to us."

Hoyt paid and took hold of a remaining bag, clutching it to his chest with one arm. Mister McAllum and Miss Olivia left the store, ringing the bell as they did so. Hoyt turned back to Diana and the remaining shoppers, tipping his hat. "Good day, ladies and gentlemen. May they see fit to bless you all."

The strange but intoxicating individual left the shop, closing the door behind.

"Weirdo," Natalie said, half whispering.

"Phew," Denny whistled.

"What was that he just said? I've never heard that before," Lorraine asked.

Sally looked to her. "What?"

"May they bless you all?"

"I have no idea," Diana replied. She watched through the window as Hoyt jumped in to the passenger side of a rusted Chevy. *'May they see fit to bless you all.*' She'd have a word at the station later and see if anyone else had heard of it, or if it had any relevance to anything.

Hoyt's words would have relevance, but in time.

# 14

Palmer roused to the sound of tapping. The blinds in the room were pulled, shielding most of the daylight outside. The sofa felt comfortable. So comfortable, it had relaxed him enough to drift away in to a light sleep. The Rest Room as they knew it at the PD was a blessing, and due to his nocturnal activities the previous night, he'd pulled rank and taken it for himself. In fact, he hadn't expected to sleep, just rest up a moment or so as the chaos around him continued.

"Sheriff?" The door tapped again. "Sheriff, you in there?"

"Yeah," he replied, clearing his throat. "Give me a minute." Palmer rubbed his face, hoping to rejuvenate his tiredness. A quick smell of his armpits detected no obnoxious odours. He rose from the couch and strolled to the door.

"Sheriff. Sorry to disturb you but the Mayor's in." Deputy Brooks stood in the doorway. He didn't look like he'd shaved for a while, but at least he looked fresh.

"Christ," Palmer sighed, "what does he want?"

Brooks raised his brows. "He wants to talk to you."

Palmer left the room, walking side by side with Brooks through the corridor.

"Any updates yet?"

Brooks shook his head. "Nothing. Feds are probing here and there, but nothing more. Their interested in Hoyt and searching Shadow Oak Farm, but that's it so far."

Anthony Brooks was young at a shade over thirty, but he'd shown so much promise since becoming Deputy. Brooks had also grown up in The Fall, and at times been ridiculed by the kids at school. Times changed, though, and nothing gave Palmer more satisfaction than seeing Brooks deliver one of his old bullies to the station. Brooks was a good kid, and one he wanted to take the Sheriff's position when he retired.

"How's morale?" Palmer asked, clenching a fist over a yawn.

"We're stretched out, as you know. The team's exhausted. We're operating on less than a skeleton crew tonight. I had to give them time off to recover."

Palmer's walk became forceful. "Who's on duty, then?"

Brooks brushed past Jeanette, who was doubling as everything now. Receptionist, cleaner, note taker, and probably a whole host of jobs she'd taken on without informing him. Palmer would give her a raise after this, when everything was finished.

"Michael and Alex are off duty now. They're coming in from eight to work the night, on the beat. Andy's back in, so I placed him in dispatch. Diana's also back, working the beat, too. That's it."

"Shit. Alright, it's do-able." They rounded a corner and approached the Sheriff's office. Through the door Palmer saw the Mayor. "Look at this guy."

Mayor Allan Shipham bore a tight, purple hoodie that revealed every inch of his girth. Across it, 'Millers Fall' stood proud in white lettering. The grey tracksuit bottoms suggested he was either dressed to exercise or relax.

Palmer entered his office. "Hey, Al. Did you run here?"

Brooks closed the door.

"You mind telling me what's going on?" Palmer gestured to a chair. All three of them sat down together.

"With what?"

"What the hell do you think?" Shipham snapped. "I got people coming up to me, asking me about daylight at night, meteors, missing people, and I have no damn idea what to tell them."

"Well, I can't fill you in on much more, because that's all that we know."

"Dammit, Mason, you have to keep me in the loop! I need to know what to say to ease my constituents concerns."

"You want a coffee?"

The Mayor glared back at Palmer. "Yes I do!" Palmer caught the wry smile from Brooks in the corner of his eye.

Palmer reached for his phone. "Yeah, can you send in three coffees please?" He looked to Shipham. "And the biscuits, too." He was going to need something to settle him down. "So, what do you want to know, Al?" he asked, placing the receiver down. "We got the residents of Glenn Avenue North, missing, without a trace. We got four officers missing, without a trace. We had a meteor crash on to Mitchum Hoyt's land last night, and guess what? It left no trace. We have a sunset every night at midnight. We have the Feds taking residence in the station. And between all of us, we haven't a damn idea what's going on."

"I heard it was five officers missing?"

"No, four. I ran one over last night on the way back from Hoyt's place."

"You did what?"

"It's okay. He's up at Willow Tree Hospital. Should be out soon, if we're lucky."

"You interrogated him yet?"

Palmer nodded. "Briefly. We'll be running him in as soon as he's discharged." There was prolonged silence between the pair from across the table.

"What? And that's it?" Shipham asked.

"Yep. That's it. Our real investigation begins when we secure Officer Renton for questioning. Until then, we're flying by the seat of our pants."

Shipham sighed. "The town's in a state. Everyone is concerned about what's happening. What should I tell them?"

"I'd advise you to explain that we're dealing with it. That's it."

"For Christ's sake, Mason. I can't leave it at that. Everyone knows there's something wrong in town and they'll be looking to me for answers. Hell, they already are."

"Sorry, sir, I can't help you with that one."

Shipham looked up. "Actually, yes you can. I'm calling a town meeting for tonight. Eight o'clock. You be there. You too, Deputy."

"Come on, Al. What do you think is going on? We don't have time for a Q and A about this."

"I don't care! You'll both be there to talk to our people. They need to be settled." Shipham stormed from the office, opening the door. Jeanette jumped, doing well to keep three cups on top of the tray she carried. Shipham looked to the chocolate biscuits and took a handful. He raised them back to Palmer. "I was doing really well until I came in here. Day four I was on. Day four on the full detox." The mayor sighed. "Be there. Eight, and not a second after."

Jeanette entered as Mayor Shipham left, placing the tray on Palmer's desk. She handed a cup first to Brooks and then to him. Palmer noticed the spare coffee and smiled to her.

"Won't you join us?"

***

After the coffee break, Sherriff Palmer and Deputy Brooks went about their business. Brooks headed to the hospital, relieving Clark of guard duty, and Palmer entertained the Feds. He spent a couple of hours at least discussing Mitchum Hoyt and his friends living up on Shadow Oak. The more they investigated Hoyt, the further away his involvement in everything appeared.

The telephone rang. "Yeah?" Palmer asked, answering it within the first ring.

"Sheriff, I have Anthony on the line," Jeanette replied.

"Put him through." The line clicked and ambience changed. "Deputy, how's things?"

"Good, sir."

"His family get there?"

"Yeah. They've been here a while now. Since before I came on duty, anyway. Listen, the doctors informed me he's ready to be discharged. I'm ringing to ask how you want to go about this?"

Palmer looked across to the Feds. "Okay. Just ask him to accompany you down here. Tell him we want to get a full statement, ask some more questions about what happened and that we need to do it as soon as possible."

"So you don't want any arrest or anything like that? The way our Agent friends have been talking, I thought I may have to, you know, read his rights."

"No, no, no, It's standard questioning at this time, Deputy. I'll get everything set up and ready, just make sure he's one hundred percent before you leave."

Palmer hung up. "Is that our man?" Davis asked.

Palmer nodded. "On his way."

## 15

Cane sat at the table, mulling over the papers with a fresh coffee. The steam swayed, rising from the polythene cup to catch his eye, so much so that he reached over and took a sip. This must have been the third drink he'd had since arriving at the Millers Fall Library a few hours ago. Frowning, he returned his gaze to the images. On the left, a town map of The Fall dated eighteen ninety eight. Of course, it had been re-drawn, but the information he needed was there. To the right, a more modern map appeared, draught by an engineer in two thousand and seven. Many of the structures existed on both maps, with only a few alterations here and there. The building he looked for had moved. The church, back in ninety eight stood central within the town, but today, it peered over the fall from a small hill on the outskirts.

He turned as a warbling, old voice made itself known. Some old fart wanted Jackie Collins, and the librarian, as professional and polite as she could be, explained that if they had it, it would be on the shelf. Cane turned back, smiling as he sipped the top of his drink.

"So," he whispered, looking at the church boundaries, "what are you now?" Not being native to this part of the world, and having yet to explore the town in any great detail, it proved difficult.

Footsteps approached across the glazed floor. "How are you doing?" The librarian asked as she approached. This woman knocked every stereotype of a librarian out of the stadium. Jeans, sweater, red hair and a genuine smile? The days of cardigans and chorded glasses had long been exercised from this town.

"Ah, I was just about to come find you..." he peered to her name tag. "Sandra. Do you have a minute?"

She looked around to an empty building, well, except for that old fart and aisles of books.

"Sure. What can I help you with?"

He gestured to the chair beside him, which she took. "I'm trying to research some of the history here in Millers Fall. I'm not local, but I'm thinking of buying property here if one becomes available. Travel, work, you know?" Sandra nodded. "Anyway, I like to learn about places before I make any decisions, and I've been going over these maps." Cane flapped the papers, making them accessible for the librarian to see. He pointed to the church. "Right here, back in eighteen, err, whenever, the church stood in the centre of town. Now, according to the newer map, it's located on the outskirts?"

"Yes, in the nineteen fifties, fifty four I think, the decision was made to build a newer, more modern building for worship. The only site for such a building was the location you can find it at now, just up on the hill. It was made bigger, to hold more people. Back during that time, though, there were more worshippers than you'll find today."

He studied the modern map. "So, what stands there today? At the site of the old church?"

"That's the police station now. They expanded to it, of course, to make it fit for purpose. Over the years it's been refurbished, built on, I can't even tell you what they've done. All I know is it looks like a police station now."

"Excuse me? Are you serving today?"

They both peered around to see the cantankerous old cow waving a book in greeting.

"You better go," Cane suggested.

The librarian smiled. "As she's already reminded me today, it's what I'm paid to do. Did I help?"

"Of course, you've been most helpful. Thank you."

He watched as she returned to her desk, and endured another ear-bashing from a less than satisfied customer. "So, you're the police station?" He folded the maps, finished his drink and threw the cup away. Whenever shit went down on these missions, the police were always there to protect the public interest. If shit was going down like he believed it would, he'd have to get arrested, to ensure he was onsite when the fan came out for it to hit.

\*\*\*

"My God. Really? Grounded all week. That's a turd." Billy expressed his opinion upon hearing Tad's punishment of their nocturnal adventures. Tad sat at his desk, skyping with his best friends. They'd both bee grounded too, but only for the weekend. Tad wondered why his Dad had to be so harsh.

"It's not going to stop me," Tad began, explaining his future plans to them. "I'm heading up there after school. I want to see where it crashed. There might be something left."

Jake shook his head. "I doubt it. If they'd found anything, it'd be gone by now. You really want to risk being grounded even more?"

"It's a risk I'm willing to take. I mean, what the hell can they do if I'm already out?"

"What about your brother? He still pounding on you?" Billy asked, scratching his cheek within the screen.

"Sam's not my brother. He's a jackoff, always has been, always will be. It makes no difference what I do, he still gonna beat me if he gets the chance."

Jake sympathized. "At least you get rid of him this year. As long as he gets his scholarship?"

"I hope so. Sooner he does one the better."

Billy reverted them back to the meteor. "So, you said we were going back up to the crash site tomorrow?"

"*We?* I don't remember saying *we*."

"Tad, we're a team. Us against the world, and all that. You think we don't want to see what's up there, either?"

Jake appeared less than enthused. "I don't know, guys. It's a little too close to that farm for my liking. Let's say that those people *did* take those guys from school. Don't you think we'd be trying our luck by being on their property?"

He had a point. Tad knew that luck was waning mighty thin at the moment, but there was something etching away in his mind that compelled him to continue. Maybe it was the mystery? Maybe it was the meteor calling to his love of science fiction? All he knew was that this was a risk worth taking.

"Nah," he replied, "they've got too much to lose. They're gonna know that the whole town suspects them, and that the police are probably taking an extra interest. I think we'll be okay to head on up there. I'm not saying they won't chase us off their property or anything like that, I'm just saying the biggest threat, for me at least, is coming home late."

Billy grinned. "I like your line of thinking. Ain't nothing to worry about. I'll bike to school tomorrow. Damn woods are too far away to walk."

"Me too," Jake added, "I just hope you're both right."

"Didn't you say you'd get us our asses kicked one day?" Tad quipped.

"Yes, but I didn't mean so soon."

# 16

Sherriff Palmer stood behind the one way glass and watched, arms folded, as Finn Renton sat behind a simple table. He'd never had to do this before, in all the years served on the force. You looked out for each other. You protected one another. He felt sympathy for the fellow officer, and useless in the situation. Finn couldn't do anything like this. Fourteen different blood samples? All in one night? You'd have to be one hell of a psycho to carry out that kind of act in such a short period. Finn just didn't have it in him.

He looked on as the officer sat there, hands clasped around a plastic coffee cup. Straight from the hospital to questioning, no stop home, no passing Go. God only knew how he must be feeling right now.

The door beside him opened. Agent Davis poked his head through. "Everything set up?"

Palmer nodded. "Good to go."

"Seeing as your running things, we thought you may want to do the questioning with Agent Welsh, here?"

Palmer looked across to Davis' buddy. "Sure. Let's get going."

\*\*\*

Both men entered the interrogation room. Finn looked up and smiled. It was clear he was nervous.

"Finn, this is Agent Welsh from the Federal Bureau of Investigation. We have some questions we'd like you to answer."

"Do I need to have a lawyer here?" Finn asked.

Welsh shook his head. "No, sir. You're not under arrest. We're just trying to piece together what happened on Glenn Avenue."

*'Wow. When you do speak, you're better at it than your buddy,'* Palmer thought.

"Okay. I want you to recall what you told me in the hospital to begin with, please?" Palmer asked, shuffling to make his ass comfortable.

Finn recounted the memories he'd had. The screaming, the light, just as he had done from beneath the lamp of the hospital bed.

"You have no recollection of how you got there?" Welsh asked.

Finn shook his head. "None. I remember knocking on the doors up there on Glenn, but that was it."

"And you don't know where you appeared?"

"No. It was just bright. I remember thinking I'd died and gone to Hell, with all that screaming. Man, that was terrifying."

Welsh took a case file he'd rested on the table and slid it across the surface to Finn. "You mind explaining this, then?" Finn took the document. "We'll give you a moment to read it. Sheriff?"

Welsh moved to the door and beckoned Palmer across. Palmer stood, making eye contact for a second with his officer. They said nothing.

"Let's give him a chance to read up on everything," Welsh explained as they stood outside. "I want to see how he reacts." Davis joined them.

"Look, he's been through enough as it is. I don't know if he'll take interrogation like this. Can't you have him tested on a polygraph?"

Davis placed a hand on his shoulder. "I'm pulling you from the interrogation." Palmer turned, ready to argue. "You're just too involved with him, and I wouldn't expect anything less. We need to be impartial towards him, and I just don't think you can do that." Davis was right, and Palmer agreed, however much he hated it. He was on Finn's side, and would be until proven otherwise. "Look, you have that town meeting to attend tonight. Go there, leave this to us. We won't do anything without contacting you. I usually don't like or care about the opinions of the local law enforcement I work with," he smiled, "but I like you. Not much, I'll admit, but I do like you. You have balls. You're not afraid to make decisions, and that goes a long way in my estimation."

Palmer said nothing. He never knew of an FBI Agent praising a law enforcer, even this slight, and didn't know how to react. Honestly, the feeling wasn't mutual.

## 17

"Okay, people, welcome. We're ready to get underway." Palmer sat atop a small stage inside town hall with Deputy Brooks to his left. To the right, Mayor Shipham took to the podium to address the residents of The Fall. Beside him sat the three remaining members of the committee, all of them with an air of self-importance, swaggering around like their shit didn't stink, well, to him anyways. Mason Palmer was paid to be Sheriff, and he did so, but kept his tongue in place with personal opinions. Margot Ridder, as upper class as she believed herself, sat proud, looking out on to the sea of faces. She still wore floral blouses and huge rimmed glasses, afraid to take the step beyond the seventies. Royston Langley pitched beside her.

Well, Royston was okay himself, but would be caught with the rest when it came to decision making. Palmer knew Langley wouldn't green light without the committee's say so, but kept himself in their good graces. He'd served Millers Fall for almost three decades now. Finally, Wes Carpenter. He managed the used cars lot across town. Palmer really didn't have much time for him, being the guy who knew everything, and knew it better than you. Even when he was wrong, he was still right, and that led to many bust-ups and arguments during committee meetings.

The audience settled from its chatter. It had been a good turn-out considering the meeting only advertised a few hours beforehand. In fact, it looked like most of The Fall made attendance. Two hundred seats were set out, one hundred on each side of an aisle, leading from the stage down to the entrance. They were full, and still people stood around the edges. The Brownings were there, Jeanette would not miss this opportunity for the world, as was Natalie Clark and her husband, Neil. The Barefords sat in the middle, Paul and Lorraine accompanied by their son Matt, his partner Nicky and their son, Noah. The good ol' boys, Terry Curtis and Buck Jeffley, The Falls resident hunters and beer swiggers. As always, they were itching for a reason to go out and shoot something. Someone caught Palmer's eye. He stood at the back, clad in a green jacket and jeans. Palmer had never seen this guy around before. Maybe he was passing through, taking an interest in all the commotion?

"This meeting has been called to discuss the recent events within our town." Mayor Shipham ruffled paper as he read over the notes he'd prepared. "Now, everyone is aware that a few days ago members of our police force disappeared, along with the residents on Glenn Avenue. At this time, we have one of the police officers currently in custody for questioning, to help us find out what happened. The remaining people, sadly, are still missing, and we are doing our utmost to locate them all."

"Come on, Al! You know where they are!" a male voice echoed from the township. They roared in unison, agreeing with the disembodied voice.

"I'm sorry, I don't quite get where you're going?"

"Don't mess with us, Mayor. We know that bunch of inbred hillbillies has them." Buck sat back in the chair, folding his arms across a hefty girth. His eyes peered out from beneath a grubby, blue cap. Palmer had a dislike to him, and his friend, Terry. Seventy percent of drunken disturbances were usually caused by this hunting duo. No matter what Palmer thought, it seemed the town people agreed.

Shipham flashed a 'help me' glance in Palmer's direction.

"Mister Jeffley, I can assure you that is not the case. They have nothing to do with it." Something was brewing. Palmer knew so. He was about to have a fight on his hands.

Buck sneered. "I expected you to say that, Sheriff. I think we all did. Seems those bastards can do whatever they want, but us law abiding citizens are where the blame lies. Am I right?"

Palmer sighed. "Mister Jeffley, I take it you're referring to the case of our missing teens?"

"Not just that, Sheriff. How about the fire out near Carson's Rock last summer, in which Pete Jakeman lost his crop? You remember that, Pete?" Buck turned his attention across the room.

"Sure do, Buck. Seems no-one was hauled in for that. I lost my god-damned livelihood during that attack. Not even the damn insurance company would pay out."

Brooks sat upright. "Hey, come on. There was no sign of foul play."

"That's right," Palmer began, "if we'd have found something we would have acted."

"Always the same story," Pete replied. "If it hadn't been for the good people of The Fall, pulling together like they always do, me, my wife and son would be living in a shelter home right about now."

Town Hall erupted in agreement. Palmer rubbed a finger across his forehead.

"Settle, please. Settle, everyone." Shipham's attempts to take control were futile.

Palmer stood up. "Alright!" he shouted, silencing the crowd and gaining their attention. "Now, I understand your frustrations, believe me."

"Sure you do!" a voice bellowed, raising a few laughs.

"I do, but the fact of the matter is this; if there's no evidence of foul play on their behalf, I can't arrest or bring charges against them." He turned to look at the committee. "I don't like that they're out there, trust me on that. The fact is, though, that they're living on a property owned by their leader. They're not committing any crime."

"Sheriff Palmer is right," Mayor Shipham added. "Whether we like it or we don't, those folks out there are living in peace. If it will settle your concerns, I will ensure that the Police Department keep a closer eye on them and their behaviour."

For once in his life, Palmer appreciated his senior. Shipham stood beside him, which meant they were unified on this at least.

"The status of the investigation is still ongoing, but you have my word we will not stop until those boys are located." Palmer took to his seat. Buck shook his head and smiled.

"What about the sky?" came a solitary voice.

Shipham looked out to his audience. "The sky? Well, um, we've made some calls, spoken to some experts in meteorology, and it is the belief that the sky illuminating at night is natural. Well, they don't know exactly what it is, but the atmosphere over our town has been monitored since the first night it occurred, and they have not reported anything out of the ordinary. This, in effect, has now been classed a natural occurrence. There is nothing but nature causing our night lights."

Sheriff Palmer sat back, unsure why he was needed. The townspeople should be tearing their mayor a new A, not the guy that's employed to protect them. He could be back at the station investigating Finn. The cell phone in his pocket rumbled. It stopped, and started again. It stopped once more. He'd all but lost Shipham's speech now. Palmer swiped the screen and pushed a button. The station had tried to call. A siren sliced through the meeting from a distance. Palmer knew it was one of his. He looked to the mayor.

"Sorry," he uttered before gesturing to Brooks. "Come on."

The officers made their way along the aisle, passing between the bodies like a modern day Moses. The stranger he'd noticed earlier had vanished.

Their footfalls echoed across the floorboards. Palmer tapped the phone and returned the call.

"What is it?" he asked.

"Sir, we got an incident!" Officer Loveridge began. "We have confirmed reports of a naked woman running through town!"

Palmer and Brooks stepped outside in to a heavy rain.

"Wait. A naked woman?" The sirens wailed a way away. "Seriously?"

"Yes. She's been reported injured, almost like how you found Finn."

Palmer's interest peaked. "Where?"

"Heading along Victoria Chase."

Palmer snapped his fingers to Brooks. "We're on our way." He ended the call. "We got another one."

Both took through the weather which had saturated the town whilst they were inside. "What?" asked Brooks.

They cantered across to the car. The rain rattled their jackets. "Like Finn."

***

The siren engaged as Sheriff Palmer and his Deputy sped through the downpour. The wipers removed a torrent of rainwater, distorting lamps illuminating the street. Through the windscreen a patrol car emerged, parked diagonally across the road. Officer York appeared before them, gesturing to slow down. Palmer killed the engine. Siren lights still engaged.

"What is it?" Palmer asked, stepping from the car.

"Take it easy. We got a standoff, but my God, she's bust up real bad."

"What happened?"

"We caught up but she became violent. Even with all that done to her, she fought us. During the struggle she removed Alex's gun."

"Christ!"

Officer York grimaced. "Looks like someone took an axe to her. Shit, how she's even alive is beyond me."

Palmer glided through the rain to their patrol car. Alex stood in the road, his palms upright at his waist in a non-confrontational stance, one learnt during basic training. Over Alex's shoulder the injured woman aimed a barrel in his direction.

101

"My God," Palmer whispered. His stomach rolled. Her abdomen was sliced from groin to jaw, and held in place by some metallic looking objects, like staples or something. Her organs rolled to the opening as black and crimson lumps of flesh, each pushing against the incision with her subtle movement. The woman's face harboured more incisions held together by silver stitches. Blood fell from her stomach, upon her thighs and down to the road. The thought of a modern day Prometheus sat in Palmer's mind. The quell of sickness churned within. "How the hell is she still standing?" He turned to Deputy Brooks. "Both of you, stay here and cover me. Call an EMT."

Brooks nodded. York un-holstered his pistol.

Palmer moved past the car and headed towards Officer Duggan. Alex turned, meeting his eyes in an instant. Palmer raised a hand, palm outward, attempting to settle any nerves. The woman emerged clearer through the downpour. His heart thudded. She'd been hacked up. The naked body harboured thick, dark scars across its entire surface. They ran horizontal and vertical, some bleeding as they mixed with the rain water. The scars continued upward, across the skin upon her neck and face. Her lips had been sliced from their corners through the cheeks. Palmer stopped beside Officer Duggan. She should be dead. She *should* be dead. No-one can suffer this kind of torture and still be standing. Her eyes appeared sunk and red as she sobbed, holding them both at gunpoint. Something rang familiar with Palmer as he gazed in to her eyes. She'd been disfigured, covered in lacerations, but still something was familiar. Then, he knew.

"Tina?" he asked. The rain rattled the tarmac. "Tina, it's me. Mason Palmer. Sheriff Mason Palmer."

"Tina?" Alex asked, his voice distained.

Palmer hushed him. "Tina, you're safe now. We mean you no harm." Tina aimed the barrel in his direction. Her intestine heaved against the stitches. Palmer raised his hands. "We mean you no harm. Come with us. You need medical assistance. We have to help you."

Tina burst in to tears, her body trembling as she sobbed. Palmer moved closer.

"Get away from me!" She screamed. He halted. Tina wiped the rain from her cheek, catching a scar and making it bleed.

"Tina."

"Don't talk! Don't do anything!" She winced, lurching forward. A cry of pain expelled from her body. The gun remained on the Sheriff. Her cries continued, deep, tortured and distressed. She coughed, whining between each gasp, before vomiting a mixture of blood and bile on to the road. The open wound revealed her stomach as it tensed.

Palmer turned away, unable to watch. The rain plastered him from every angle. It fell cool and refreshing, almost as a pure element destined to wash away this horror. Tina finished. About her on the road's reflective surface sat a torrent of blood and flesh.

Palmer looked to her once more. "Are you...."

"Get back!" she screamed, uncaring for Palmer's concern.

"Tina, we can help."

Tina stood upright, sighing with each movement. Mucus hung from one nostril. "No. No, you can't." She turned the barrel and pressed it against her temple.

"Tina, no!"

"He knows. He is the one who knows. Go to the farm. For the love of God, save this town."

Blood exploded before the shot of the gunfire popped. The blast echoed through the street. Tina's head shattered. The right side vanished to a spray of liquid and matter. Palmer ducked as the lifeless body dropped the gun and slumped to the floor.

"Oh my God! EMT! EMT now!" Palmer screamed, but it was too late. Pink flesh lay in clumps across the tarmac. An eye lay hanging from the wound. Brooks' footfalls within the puddles brought Palmer back to the situation.

"I don't believe it," he whined, placing a hand across his mouth.

Palmer looked at the body. That wasn't Tina, at least not now. *That* had been assembled like a jigsaw, in his mind. Tina's body resembled a deranged experiment. Somewhere, a mad doctor was laughing maniacally. His creation had worked. Whoever did this was beyond insane, still at large, and according to Tina, connected to the farm. There was only one farm currently in question. Shadow Oak.

***

The patrol cars screamed through the trees. Sheriff Palmer and Deputy Brooks charged through the rain. Mister McAllum stood upon the porch.

"Where is he?" Palmer snapped. Unkempt people appeared in the buildings windows. Men bore beards of various shades and lengths. Woman wore simple dresses. For the first time Palmer saw the true extend of the clan Mitchum Hoyt harboured. Twenty, maybe even thirty people appeared around the house. Some loomed from the darkness. One man stood there, his face shrouded with a burlap sack. Chaos engulfed Shadow Oak. Patrol cars, sirens, bodies. This was a raid.

"Where is he?" Palmer screamed again. McAllum pointed toward the open door.

The Sheriff pushed through the bodies in to the house and past Altman. Candles illuminated the path. "Hoyt!"

"I'm not a hard man to find." Hoyt appeared beneath a candle, hands in pockets. "You come on to my land, distress my people and holler my name. I'm taking it you have a warrant?"

"Mitchum Hoyt, you're coming with me."

"On what charge?"

Palmer pushed Hoyt against the wall and turned him around, ignoring the question. Hoyt laughed.

"Deputy. Handcuffs."

"But sir, he's not under…."

104

"Damn it, Anthony, just give me the God-damned cuffs!"

Brooks handed them across. Palmer snapped them around Hoyt's wrists, turned him about and pushed him towards the exit. Both officers flanked Hoyt, each grasping an arm.

Hoyt chuckled as they passed his people. "Our efforts have been in vain, my friends."

They passed back out to the patrol cars. A plethora of backwoods eyes watched as the three emerged on to the porch. McAllum and Altman strode across, their demeanour one of intent.

"No!" Hoyt glared to his followers. McAllum's eyes widened. "No, Mister McAllum." Palmer peered out in to the rain. Officers Duggan and York had their pistols drawn toward the bearded clan. Along with Brooks, Palmer encouraged Hoyt to descend the porch to the sodden floor. "Take care of our people until I return."

They reached the vehicles without incident. Brooks opened the rear door as Palmer pushed Hoyt's head inside. Slamming the wing, Palmer turned back to the farmhouse. People engulfed the grounds, both inside and out. Simple clothes, simple haircuts, everything about them seemed so easy and carefree. All stood in the rain, watching the officers take their leader in to custody. Mister McAllum grasped the porch banister and leaned out in to the downpour. The man hidden by the burlap sack stood motionless, his head tilted to one side.

Officers Duggan and York retreated to their own vehicle as Brooks fired the engine and span the car around. Soon enough they bounded along the track to the main road, and headed back toward The Fall.

"I'm needed for what?" Hoyt's voice drifted from the rear. The tone he used, the way he spoke, was mesmerising.

"That's not for discussion at this time," Palmer replied. "It's routine questioning." Raindrops fell in blobs against the windscreen.

"Something in your voice tells me that's not the whole story."

"That was not a negotiation, Mister Hoyt, it was a statement. There will be no further discussion."

Hoyt chuckled. "As you wish, Sheriff."

The road back appeared a great deal longer. Weights tugged against Palmer's eyelids. Damn, when did he last sleep properly? Rubbing his eyes he sighed out. It had been a long time ago, for sure. Get Hoyt into interrogation, grab a coffee, throw out a few questions, then this time go home. Sleep in his own bed, that's what he needed.

"Is that the right time?"

Palmer looked to the dashboard. Eleven fifty nine. "Yes, that's correct."

Hoyt shuffled on the seat. "Get ready, my friends."

"For w-"

A burst of orange light rippled between the clouds. The vehicle juddered. Brooks slowed as the car quaked, ready to give out.

"Anthony? What the hell?"

"It's not me, sir."

The siren blasted twice before the car stalled. Everything died. The dashboard lights, radio, headlamps, even the comms system. The sky expelled the bright, summer light as they sat there, unable to move. Hoyt laughed. This time, he didn't let up. The car shook. Palmer reached out and grabbed the door handle. They rocked from side to side as the road quaked beneath them. Hoyt's crazed laugh continued. They swayed back and forth, thrown around like riding some rollercoaster.

"Is this what you want?" Hoyt screamed above the earthquake.

"What are you talking about?!" Palmer snapped.

"This is it! The first step! It's starting!"

"What?"

"There's no turning back! This is it! This is it!"

The vehicle settled. The tremors diminished. The summer light faded, returning the sky once more to darkened cloud. Palmer sat there, unable to process what had happened, listening to the silence.

"You can drive now." Hoyt smiled in the rear view mirror.

"What? The car's de-"

Light flashed from the dashboard. The radio fizzed to life. With a flicker of effort the headlamps returned, illuminating the road. The engine coughed and returned to with a roar. Palmer looked to Brooks. His expression, mouth open, eyebrows raised, suggested he was spooked.

Palmer turned to face Hoyt. Hoyt smiled, his cherub features bulbous through the beard.

"Mister Hoyt, you and I are going to have a serious chat, all night if we have to."

Palmer burst through the door. Hoyt wondered in tow, gripped again by Deputy Brooks. Officer Loveridge and Jeanette stood within the reception area, watching as they passed. Only now did he feel angry. Hoyt was up to something, and sure as hell tied in to everything one way or another. Images of Tina, slashed open with her guts attempting an escape, hacked almost beyond recognition, exploding in to red mist, engulfed his mind. Something scared her, enough to take her own life. Finn languished in custody, one of his own, taken for questioning. Did he experience anything like Tina? He was covered in blood, most of which was not his own. Traces of Tina's had been found upon him. God, if this was right, what the hell we're the others going through, and where were they? They had to be close. No-one could travel any distance, especially Tina, after the torture she'd been put through. Things were tying together. Tina suggested they head to the farm, likely for some kind of answer. 'He knows,' she had told them, and there was only one 'he,' the man who now wandered the corridor behind.

Palmer barged through double doors, rattling their frames. Davis and Welsh appeared ahead.

"Whoa, whoa, whoa. What is this?" Davis asked. "Are you insane?"

Palmer ignored him. "Where's Finn?"

The Agent's cantered beside them. "Don't ignore me, Sheriff. I asked you a question!"

Palmer smashed Davis to the wall, taking grip of his jacket. "You listen to me! I've put up with your bullshit long enough! I've got one officer locked up on the suspicion of murder. I just watched another blow her God-damned brains across the street after threatening to kill us, her colleagues, her team. Her damn body had been hacked up worse than a London prostitute in Victorian England. Before she died, she told me this son-of-a-bitch knew. She told me he knew something about the world of shit that's breezed across this town. You wanted him, sir, you got him."

Davis snarled. "You haven't even charged the guy! There's nothing to charge him with!"

Palmer turned to Hoyt. "That's right. Mister Hoyt accompanied us of his own free will. Isn't that right, Mister Hoyt?"

Hoyt chuckled. "Of course it is, Sheriff. I am always eager to help our law enforcement."

"Sir?" Palmer turned to see Officers York and Duggan enter the fray. Between them stood the stranger he'd noticed at the town meeting, his hands cuffed. "We found this guy at the farm, just as we left. It would appear he had an interest in Shadow Oak, too." Alex nudged their prisoner. "Resisted arrest, attempted to flee, we thought he may be of some interest."

"Alex, get him to the cell, I'll question him later. Michael, I want the pathologist called and at the hospital, now. I want to know exactly what happened to Tina, and before dawn. You got it?"

Michael looked to the Sheriff. "Sheriff, I don't know if-"

"That's a god-damned order, York! Get her here now! Deputy, make sure it happens."

Brooks nodded. "Yes, sir, but I think you need to maybe look at things with a clearer mind before you continue."

"What?" Palmer set himself to explode.

"I'll make Mister Hoyt comfortable, down in interrogation room one. You three," Brooks dared, addressing his seniors, "need to grab a coffee or something first."

Palmer glanced across to Welsh, who met his gaze behind reflected lenses. What the hell was he doing? He'd never flipped like this before, not ever. Palmer relaxed the cloth he grasped, sighed and stepped away, releasing the Agent. Davis adjusted the jacket and shrugged his shoulders.

"We're going to have a serious conversation, Sheriff."

"You should do," Hoyt began, "that looked incredibly unprofessional."

"Shut your mouth," The Sheriff ordered.

"Alright, that's enough." Brooks pushed Hoyt along the corridor. Palmer watched the cult leader pass, glaring back.

"They're coming." Palmer frowned, catching Hoyt's whisper. Hoyt peered back, his grin now one of malevolence. "They're coming."

Deputy Brooks vanished beyond another set of doors with the suspect. Palmer looked to the floor.

"Final warning, Palmer. You screw with me like that again, not only will I remove you from the investigation I'll make damn sure your badge and gun remain in my possession permanently." Davis leant closer. "We're in charge now."

Palmer quelled the anger resurging inside. What was the point? Nothing he could do now. For the first time in his career emotion had got the better of him, and he'd paid for it.

Davis moved in to his eye-line. "Now, I'm gonna put your little outburst down to exhaustion, you got that? I suggest you go get some rest."

"What did you do with Finn?"

"Don't worry about him," Welsh began, "he's co-operating fully. We want to keep him further. There's still some gaps he needs to fill in."

Davis laid a heavy hand on Palmer's shoulder. "Go. Rest up. If we need you, we'll call."

Palmer watched as the Agents vanished from the corridor. Something pounded behind his eye. Great, a headache coming on, too. He turned to find Alex, Michael and their prisoner.

"Look, sorry guys. I didn't mean to bust your asses like that. Just, make sure the results of the investigation are with me before dawn. We owe it to Tina to find out what happened."

Michael smiled. "Will do, Sheriff."

"Did you get an ID on this guy?" Palmer gestured towards the prisoner.

"You know what? If you ask me I'll just tell you," the prisoner jumped in.

"Richard Parks. Taking a vacation from Port Sandown, at least according to his driving licence," Alex explained.

"Port Sandown, eh? Okay, throw him in, but grab his prints and everything first. Run a full history."

"Sure thing." Alex gestured for Rick to move. "Hey, Sheriff." Palmer turned to Alex.

"Yeah?"

"After he's booked in, you, um, you want us to run out to her husband? You know? Tina?"

Palmer closed his eyes and nodded. "Yeah. Yeah I think you should. Might give him and the family some closure, if nothing else. But don't breath a word of her condition to him, you understand?"

"Got it."

"Do me a favour, though. Just run out past the farm and let your sirens go. I want Hoyt's people to know we're still about."

Palmer watched as the officers left the corridor, ready to run the errands he'd asked. He removed the hat, sighed and ran a palm across his hair. Let the Feds have their fun with Hoyt. He'd run them in circles, then they'd ask for help. It was almost a given to anyone who knew the crazy bastard.

Palmer turned and wandered to his office. He'd rest up soon, but not before he grabbed that coffee.

## 19

Tad roused from a light slumber. His leg tingled from the cold, hanging from the edge of the bed. From across the room an intermittent beep sounded. Tad rolled, drew his leg in to the warmth and exhaled. As he woke, the recognition of an incoming call from the laptop registered. "What?" He wandered to the desk, rubbing his eyes. After tapping the keyboard, Billy appeared on screen.

"Billy, you know what time it is? It's...." he paused. "I don't even know what time it is."

"Tad my man, I gotta tell you! Cops just came tearing down my street, sirens going, lights flashing! Man, they moved faster than my granddad with the shits!"

Tad yawned. "Billy. Really? You woke me up at..." he looked in the lower right hand of the screen. "Three twenty four! You woke me up at three twenty four! And for cop cars passing by your place?"

"Let me finish. My old man just came in from work, said he passed them on the road. He said they headed out to the farm. To the crash site."

Billy caught his attention. "What are they doing out there?"

"I don't know, but I'm going to find out. You coming?"

Tad sighed. "Bill. Did you even learn anything from last night?" Billy, ever the adventurer. He'd probably grow up to be the real life Indiana Jones.

"Yeah. I learned there's still stuff going on up there! You in?"

"Look, I'm in deep with my parent over this already. They even find out I've been talking to you now and I'll probably get grounded until our prom. Can't you wait until tomorrow? After school like we planned?"

"Hell no! It's all gonna be over by then. You want some other douche to steal our fame?"

"Is this what it's all been about?" Tad's eyes rolled. "You want to be famous?"

"Not just that. I don't want anyone to go steal our hard work."

The chair creaked as Tad leant back. "What about Jake? What did he say?"

"Jake had the sense not to answer me."

"Well, I'm answering, and I'm saying no. nothing personal, Billy-boy, I'm sticking to the plan. At least I have a reason for being late home tomorrow. Mom knows I sometimes stay behind and help feed the fish in the science labs."

Truth was, he really wanted to go. He wanted to know everything that was happening out there in the woods. If caught by his parents, though, he'd be screwed for eternity. He was playing a poker face. If Billy knew he expressed even one percent in his being to head out at this hour, Billy would convince him somehow.

After a brief pause Billy shrugged. "Alright, I'll go see what's happening for myself. No hard feelings, huh?"

"No, of course not. Meet me in the food hall tomorrow before class. Tell me what you find."

"No problem, Tad." Billy smiled. "May the force be with you."

"And you."

The call ended. Tad grasped the screen and flipped it down. He shuffled in to the bathroom, took a piss and went back to bed without washing his hands.

As sleep evaded him, his mind conjured an image of Billy, huffing his way to the woods on a bike. Damn, he was brave, if he did go. Out there in the middle of the night, and on your own? Some strange cult of peace loving weirdo's only a stone throw away? Police? Screw that. Billy's parents wouldn't give a shit that he was up to no good again, but Tad knew his Dad would scream and shout until a coronary stopped him. No, screw that, good and proper. Billy could tell him what happened tomorrow.

## 20

Sheriff Palmer stood above an open grave. The rain teemed down upon the mourners as the coffin lowered in to the soil. Flowers rattled within rain drops. A breeze gusted against his clothes. Words were uttered somewhere, which he paid little attention to. Deputy Brooks stood at his side, both watching as Tina said her final farewell. Thunder rippled through the clouds. A strange, orange light pulsed across the sky. Brooks kicked Palmer's shoe, and gestured upward. Palmer nodded.

"…and yes, my friends, the day will come when I can no longer help you. When that day arrives, you will have no one left to blame but yourselves." The Pastor laughed, throwing his head to the sky. His bible reached to the heavens. The sky bled orange, stretching across the horizon.

"You are damned! Not by the God almighty, not even by yourselves, but by them!"

He lowered his head, only he wasn't a Pastor. It was Mitchum Hoyt. Hoyt cackled through the rain. "They're coming."

Tina burst from the coffin, shattering the lid in to a thousand splinters. She reached to Palmer with bloodied hands. He stumbled back, falling to the sodden grass. The gun holster was empty. Tina crawled upon him, her remaining hair matted to the missing part of her exposed skull. A pale, dead palm grasped his leg, using his body to pull closer. Lumps of pink flesh tumbled on to his clothing. She squealed and cawed, revealing a mouth of shark's teeth. Her twisted features grinned. Palmer screamed…

"Everything alright, sir?" Brooks' voice passed through the door. Palmer found himself in the Rest Room once more, and not at a funeral. He sighed, wiping sweat from his forehead.

"Yeah. Yeah I'm good. What time is it?"

"Four forty five."

"Damn it." Well, a few hours sleep is better than none, even if you are haunted by dead colleagues. "What's up?" he asked, rubbing his face to get going.

"It's Hoyt." Palmer's stomach dropped.

*'They're coming.'*

Brooks continued. "He's playing games. Got the Feds running around like blue-assed flies. I've been sent to summon you. They need your help."

Palmer grinned as he stood and stretched. "What can I do?"

"It's Hoyt's request. He said he's only willing to speak with you and Diana."

"Alright. Hey, listen. We got the report on Tina yet?"

"The coroner's there as we speak. She's been working at the hospital a couple of hours now. You really owe her one, you know? Dragging her out of bed to haul ass down here like that?"

"Yeah. Yeah, I'll see her. Tell the Feds I'll be right there."


Hoyt perched behind the desk, his hands clasped upon the surface. He appeared as a naughty school child, caught by the teachers for lighting cherry bombs in the toilets, or something like that. Palmer and Diana received their briefing from the Agents, or 'Dickwads' as they were becoming known around the station. Palmer and Diana had their own brief discussion before entering. This time it really was the Sheriff's show, but whether Davis and Welsh liked it was another question.

Palmer opened the door allowing Diana to enter first. Both clasped a cup of fresh coffee as they headed to the desk.

Hoyt looked to them through strands of long, unclean hair. "Good morning."

The chairs squeaked across the tiled surface. "Good morning, Mister Hoyt." Palmer placed his cup on the desk. "They treating you well?"

Hoyt chuckled. "I cannot complain, Sheriff, I cannot complain."

Palmer leant upon the surface. "Okay, you know why you're here, correct?"

Hoyt nodded. "Indeed I do."

"Now, for whatever reason, you wanted to speak to Officer Trent and myself. We're accommodating people here at the Millers Fall Police Department, but know this; any more games and you will be arrested for wasting police time and obstructing a police investigation. Do I make myself clear?"

"As clear as a crystal, sir."

"Good. Then we have an understanding. Now, first and foremost, I want you to tell me why a witness would claim to be injured whilst on your property? And I'm not talking a graze from a walk in the woods, or even a broken bone from fooling around in one of the dilapidated buildings on your property. I'm talking life threatening injury caused by the hand of another."

"I have no idea." Hoyt leaned back, folding his arms.

Palmer mirrored the action. "What? That's it? You have 'no idea?' Sorry Mister Hoyt, but that just isn't good enough."

"Sheriff, it's the only explanation I have."

Palmer looked to Diana.

"Mister Hoyt," she began, clasping her hands together, "I don't know how serious you think this situation may be. We are investigating a serious crime in which you have been implicated. Even though you're not under arrest, we are interviewing you under caution. You may harm your defence if you fail to co-operate."

Hoyt release a laugh. "And you think I've not already been damaged by my implication, on unfounded evidence?"

"We have a witness who named you and your property as agitators toward her injury."

Hoyt leant forward. "So, do I take it you will be arresting me on word-of-mouth?"

A knock came from the door. Palmer turned to see the tired face of Officer York peek around. "Sir. Can we have a minute please?"

116

Palmer turned. "We will be back."

Hoyt smiled. "I count the minutes."


"What is it?" Palmer asked, entering the corridor with Diana. Michael stood with Alex and both Agents.

Welsh handed across a document. "It's the report on your officer. Tina."

Palmer took it without speaking. The first page or so he waded past, getting to the part he wanted.

The report was staggering. Such brutality. The pain she experienced must have been unlike anything experienced by anyone. It read like a depraved horror novel, each page more horrendous than the last. For the first time, a stinging sensation prickled his eyes. This was unlike anything he'd ever found. This was first of its kind, of that there was no doubt.


Palmer re-entered the interrogation room. Diana blubbered in the corridor, comforted by Michael and Alex had broken their façade of tough guys. Hoyt remained seated, although the grin had vanished.

Palmer sat, dropped the document on the surface of the table and rubbed his face. "You need to start talking, Mister Hoyt."

"Sheriff, I've told you everything I know."

Palmer nodded. "Is that so? Okay, let's see if you can help solve this, then. This," he said, waving the document at Hoyt, "is a coroner's report. You know what one of these is?"

"I find it very insulting you should speak to me in this manner. Not only have I been branded a cult leader, and abductor and hillbilly, but now you're questioning my intelligence?"

Palmer remained calm, his voice soft and unthreatening. "At this moment in time, Mister Hoyt, I don't give a rat's ass how I make you feel. What I want is your opinion on what I'm about to read. Can you at least help me with that?"

Hoyt nodded. "Of course. If I can, that is."

Palmer ruffled the papers, finding the beginning. "Okay. Let's begin. This is a report written on the state of a body lying on the slabs up at Willow Tree Hospital. Now, usually the information within these is confidential, but I'm about to break that in order to have your opinion. The deceased person was an officer from our department."

"You have my deepest condolences." Hoyt's expression at least appeared sincere.

"Yeah, well, your condolences won't bring her back, and that's not what I'm talking to you for. I'm going to read you part of this, and get your take on events. Ready?"

"I am."

Palmer cleared his throat. "The major organs remain intact, despite there being considerable length of intestine removed from the body. The bonding agent used to seal parts of the incision, as well as the component of the staples holding parts together, is one of which is unknown, and will undergo investigation via the periodic table. The intestine itself appears to have been removed with great skill, which may suggest some knowledge of procedures in this area. Traces of skin have been found inside the body. From the state of the internal organs, it is my belief that they have been removed and re-attached, although this has been done with little skill, care or attention. The liver and pancreas, for example, appear to be detached..." Palmer stopped. It was killing him.

"Are you okay, Sheriff?" Hoyt asked.

"Fine. Anyway, where was I? Yes. The skin across the entire body has been removed, and reattached with the same bonding agent stated previous. My belief is that the skin has been sliced, for reasons unknown, and re-applied. The stitching, however, appears primitive and likely done to fit back upon the body." Palmer closed the document. The tremble from his throat itched.

"That is truly deplorable," Hoyt whispered. His head lowered.

"Mister Hoyt, this is only part of it. It goes on to say that, regardless of her injuries, she died from a single bullet wound to the head. Now, I witnessed the moment she took her life. Before pulling the trigger she told us to head to your farm, and that you knew. Now, can you see why we're so interested in speaking with you?"

Hoyt leaned closer. "Sheriff. My land is vast. I cannot police it myself. All I can do is ensure that my people are protected, that is all. I can confirm to you now that this horrendous, horrendous attack has nothing to do with me."

Anger overshadowed Palmer's emotion. "I don't believe you."

Hoyt chuckled. "It makes no odds to me if you believe what I say. No, sir, it was not me," he whispered. "It's them."

"Sheriff!" Diana burst through the door. "Come quick!" He turned.

Hoyt rose from the desk like some kind of messiah. "They're here."

Palmer slammed the door, ensuring the lock engaged. "What is it?" They raced along the corridor.

"I don't know."

Through corridors and doors they ran, heading to the holding cells. They opened the final set of pine doors, walking in to a corridor that saw both Feds with Officers York, Duggan and Loveridge. All pointed their firearms towards an open door. Palmer raced across, drawing his own gun. Through the open bars sat Finn, resting against the far wall. Trails of blood swayed across its white surface. Finn's hands soaked in crimson ooze, one that spooled to a puddle where he sat.

"He's gone crazy!" Agent Davis snapped.

Finn chuckled, his head raising as he did so. Tatters of flesh flapped where cheeks once existed.

"You want to know what happened on Glenn Avenue?" The tattered body sat upright, his head hanging to the side. "It's something no one can explain, not even me. My mind, it's full of images of dread, terror and death." Finn tapped his temple. "These are images I can never un-see. That was an experience that will stay with me forever. And I know now. I know because I can feel them, like a sense of some kind. I feel them inside my mind. They're angry, and they will make us suffer." Finn jolted. Blood spewed in to the air, turning the cell to a slaughter house. He screamed, one of dread that tingled Palmer's skin to gooseflesh. Finn stood, rolling and leaning against the wall.

"What the crap!" Loveridge gasped.

Finn rolled. He bonded to the wall, as though gravity had shifted, and squirmed along its surface leaving patches of blood where he writhed.

"Holy Mary, Mother of God!" Welsh gasped.

Finn rolled upwards, towards the ceiling. The cell filled with his screams. Rolling on to his back, he looked directly to the officers. "It's too late!" Blood gushed from his eyes. "They're here."

Finn grimaced, arching his back. The cell fell quiet. He dropped to the floor, splashing to the excessive puddle spilled from his body. The ground trembled. Palmer looked to the floor. Energy struck the officers, knocking them down. Blinding, white light coursed through the corridor. Palmer pushed up on his arm, shielding his eyes with the left. A silhouette approached, breaking the light in to shafts around his shadow. The shadow laughed. Mitchum Hoyt.

"I told you, but no-one listened." Hoyt approached, stepping across the officers writhing on the floor. "Now, you've made them very angry. So angry, in fact, that I don't know if I can appease them anymore. I will do my best, though, even as you show me disrespect and ungratefulness. I warn you. I warn all of you. Leave me and my followers alone. We live a simple life away from all of you. This is your final warning. Leave us be, and we will keep them at bay." Palmer looked up as the madman squatted down. "Sheriff, as I am not under arrest, and free to leave when I wish, I tell you now that I am finished. I will return to my farm, where I'll continue to live in isolation away from you. However, should you discover any evidence in which you need me to help, I will of course co-operate fully." The light hurt Palmer's eyes. Hoyt looked about, like it didn't even phase him. "I am truly sorry for your loss, of that I am most sincere."

The light dwindled and died, leaving Palmer in the company of his fellow officers. Hoyt vanished with the aura.

Palmer lay there as liquid gurgled from Finn's throat. He pushed up on his palms.

"Shit! What the hell was that?!" Michael asked.

Palmer ignored the comment and stood. "Come on! Help me!" He waded in to the cell and dropped down beside Finn. Finn lay there, saturated in his own blood. "Come on, Finn!" Palmer barked. He reached down pushing in to the warm, red liquid staining Finn's throat. No pulse. "Dammit!" Peering across his shoulder, the officers and Agents were on the move. "Diana! Go! Get an EMT! Now!" He turned back, staring at the semi closed eyes of his dying officer. The cuff of his sleeve moved down as he cleared the blood around his mouth and nose.

"You want me to chase Hoyt?" a voice he barely recognised asked.

"No! Not yet! Help me, here."

Palmer locked his hands in place above Finn's chest, leant down, and administered fifteen compressions. Palmer leant in, pinched his nose, opened the mouth and exhaled a rescue breath. Finn's chest expanded. Palmer drew in through his nose and breathed again, before returning to his knees. Finn remained lifeless. "Shit! Come on!" Fifteen more compressions rocked his body, followed by another two rescue breaths.

"Sir, it will be quicker if we take him," Diana's voice explained from behind.

Finn coughed. His mouth expelled blood with each lurch.

"You did it!" Alex whispered.

"Finn. Finn? Can you hear me?" Palmer leant across the body, peering in to Finn's eyes. Finn gasped, raising a bloodied hand to him.

Palmer grasped it. "Loveridge. Get him to the hospital. Sirens all the way."

"Yes, sir."

By the time Finn sat upright, a wheelchair had been located and he'd been whisked out to the lot, then to the hospital. What felt like a decade later, the cell had been cleaned, the officers back on duty and the Agents gone.

Palmer sat in his office, having contacted Sergeant Harris. The plan was simple. Kim, Andy, Clark and Harris himself would pair together and keep guard at the hospital. If the events within the cell happened again he'd need someone there. That is, of course, if Finn made it.

## 21

"It looks like winter arrived early this morning out there in The Fall. Heavy fog is disrupting routes in and out of Millers Fall, so much so that the MET office has issued a severe travel warning. If you're heading out, take extra care today. It's not going to be nice and it doesn't show any sign of letting up."

Tad stepped in to the kitchen, fresh, clean and ready for school. The radio continued with the discussion about fog that settled across Millers Fall during the night.

"Good morning, honey," his Mom said, placing two slices of toast in a toast rack.

"Morning."

Sam sat at the table eating cereal. Tad joined him, and reached for his old friend, Count Chocula.

"School's off." Sam informed him.

"What?" The cereal rustled from the box to his bowl.

"Exactly what I said, dipshit."

"Do you have to talk like that?" Tad saw the distain in Mom's face.

Sam ignored her. "School is out, today. What was it they said on the radio, Mom? Teacher's couldn't get in."

"It's the fog. People are struggling to get in and out of town."

Tad flicked his eyebrows up. "Excellent." He sat in silence. The sound of cereal grinding between teeth engulfed the table. If school was out, he could head across to Billy and see what he found up at the farm. Jake would probably be there, too.

"So, what are you both doing today?" Mom asked.

Sam shrugged. "I thought we were grounded?"

"You are, but I need you both outta here. I got the ladies coming around for coffee."

Sam grunted. "Do you think Dad would appreciate that?"

Mom leant against the counter, crossing her arms. "I don't care what your Father thinks. I make decisions around here, too."

"Could have fooled me."

Mom stepped across and threw a heavy palm at Sam's head. Cereal exploded across the table.

"Jesus! Mom!"

"You bastard! Get the hell out! I don't want to see you until tonight."

Tad pushed back from the table as milk seeped through his jeans. Sam launched his bowl, smashing it against the wall.

"Get out!" she screamed.

He stormed from the kitchen. A moment later the front door slammed, rattling the frame.

Tad lost his appetite. He could see tears well in Mom's eyes. Great. What a start to the day. Without saying a word he left, grabbing his coat from the end of the banister.

The fog attacked with freezing, invisible blades. For a moment Tad considered returning inside and grabbing a hat, but didn't want to face his Mom again. Damn, it was thick out here. A vehicle passed, but the headlights didn't appear until they were almost upon him. Visibility must have been two feet at the most. The fallen cloud hung about him. Mist swirled with the passing breeze. "This is gonna be more difficult than I planned."

Tad walked to the side of the house and removed his bike from beneath a sheet of tarpaulin. As he cleared the cover and sat on the saddle, a thought struck him. He pulled the cell from his pocket and called Billy, who failed to answer. Instead of leaving a message he'd just head across there. The fog would slow him down, but not much.

The fog was as bad as they made out on the radio. Tad often rode with his earphones in, but today was different. He knew The Fall like the back of his hand, but didn't risk cycling out in to the road unable to see the hidden traffic. The fog had a chill to it. Cold moisture passed across his face as he rode the sidewalks, unwilling to risk the road. Sam was out here somewhere, but he didn't care. Hopefully he'd run out in front of an Arctic, save him and his parents the hassle.

In no time, Tad peddled on to Billy's street, and through the gloom approached the letterbox out front of his home. Plastered in bright, red paint, it was hard to miss.

Tad pulled on to the lawn and dropped the bike. The grass, covered in dew, slipped beneath his feet as he jogged across the yard and up on to the porch. His knuckle rattled the door, and a brief moment of concern crossed his mind. Was it too early? Tad pulled the cell from his pocket. 09:14. Monday morning. Half the world would be up by now. Through the door the sound of shuffling emerged. A blurred shadow appeared through the frosted glass, and a second later the door opened. Billy's father appeared, still half-asleep by the looks of it.

"Ah shit!" The balding, overweight man turned from Tad. "Billy! You're late! You'll get me called to the school again!"

"Oh no, no," Tad interrupted, sensing his friend about to receive a pounding. "School has been cancelled. The weather is too bad. I was wondering if Billy was okay to come out instead?"

Billy's father rubbed his neck. "It's cancelled?"

"Yes, sir."

The man popped his head out in to the morning. "Damn, it is bad. What are you going to be up to?"

Tad hadn't thought that far ahead. "To be honest, I'm not too sure. I was just thinking go back to mine and play video games, or something?"

"Hold on." Billy's Dad left the door, leaving Tad out in the cold, still. Tad bobbed on the spot as the cold air got to him.

"C'mon, Bill," he whispered, rubbing his arms.

Billy's Dad appeared at the door again. "Sorry, Tad. Seems he's up and gone already. I bet the dumbass has gone to school."

Tad smiled. "Okay. If you see him, tell him to call me, if that's okay?"

"Will do. You take it easy out there, okay?"

Tad left the porch and crossed the grass to his bike. "Sure will. Thank you."

He pulled the cycle up. Something didn't feel right. He scoured the phone for Jake's number and pressed call. No answer.

"Great." Tad looked around, pondering what to do. "To hell with it." The bike set in to motion as he peddled. The last time they spoke, Billy was heading up to Shadow Oak Farm. A strange feeling nestled in Tad's stomach. What if Billy went there and didn't come back?

# 22

Rick sat alone in the interrogation room, as he had done since being arrested. At first, the comfort of a room instead of a cell had been appealing, but sat here all night and most of the morning had been very unprofessional. He'd heard commotion at some point but couldn't remember when. He'd nodded off and it had woken him, that all he knew.

Across the table two vacant chairs awaited someone's arrival. The beard emerging from his throat itched like hell. He cussed for not shaving at the last opportunity.

The door opened, and in walked the Sheriff.

"Mister Parks," he began, dropping a file to the table and closing the door, "my name is Mason Palmer, and I'm the Sheriff here for Millers Fall."

His demeanour suggested he knew. Maybe not everything, but something.

"Usually I'd say 'nice to meet you,' but under the circumstances…"

Palmer smiled. "Of course. So, let's cut right to the chase. What are you doing here in my town?"

Rick shrugged. "Looking for a home. I've heard many good things about Millers Fall, and I want to move from Port Sandown. It's too busy, you know? Boats, fishing, it's just not my thing anymore."

"I understand." Palmer nodded. Rick knew he was playing. "Only problem is, you don't live in Port Sandown, do you?"

Rick shuffled. "Oh, and what gives you that impression?"

"We checked your address, and spoke to some of our colleagues out there. Very good people they are, out in the coastal regions. Needless to say, they were happy to help. Seems that a ten minute search of their systems provided us with everything we needed to know."

"Is that so?" Rick quipped.

Palmer puffed his cheeks and nodded. "Yep. Yes, it is. It would appear that your address is actually a property owned and maintained by one Phillip Hartman. Not Richard Parks. However, Mister Hartman was greatly concerned by this whole, how should we say, 'mix up.' And…" the Sheriff chuckled, "it would appear that Mister Richard Parks is a janitor with the Port Sandown Police Department."

Palmer bellowed, his body shaking as the laughter expelled from his abdomen.

"Shit." The cat was out of the bag now.

"Your identification is very convincing, I'll give you that." The Sheriff took hold of himself, sighing as he returned to formalities. "But we know it's not real, just like your name isn't real. In fact, I have your name written on this document just here, along with the prints you gave. Seems you're serving, but where about I have no idea." Palmer waved the paper. "You want to read it?" The sheet glided across the surface. Rick looked down, studying the details. He breezed over the text. Palmer became impatient. Clasping his hands, he leaned on to the table. "Listen, Rick," he emphasised, "I'm having a bad week. In fact, it's a turd of a week. You ever have one of them? A week that's just so bad, you'd happily give your left hand for it to be over and done with?"

Rick looked to him. "Sheriff, you have no idea." He smiled.

Palmer returned the gesture. "Last week I dealt with dog fouling and an incident with spray paint. That's usually as heavy as it gets around here. Little things, you know, jaywalking, littering, that kind of thing. This week, well, I've been dealing with missing people, missing police officers, orange skies at night, possible murders, a backwoods cult, and a town that would happily begin burning women at the stake to get some answers. I'll admit, this was the last thing I thought I'd be dealing with when I took the job. So please, for both our sakes, tell me who you are and what you're doing here." Rick dropped the paper and leant back in his seat. "Mister Parks, this town is scared, and I still have no answer as to what is going on. I believe you do, and if you're a civil servant of some kind, I'm asking you to remember why you took that job and the good your information can do here, for my town."

Rick pursed his lips and looked to the side. "Alright, Sheriff, but you may not like the answer."

Palmer nodded. "I'm listening."

"When your boys picked me up, I had a bag. I need it, and the contents inside."

Palmer did as requested, and returned to Rick no longer than ten minutes later clutching the bag. Rick took it without a thank you, opened the zip and emptied the contents on top of the table.

"Did your people book this in?" he asked, as Palmer returned to the seat.

"Yep. All of it."

"So, I take it you're referring to this?"

Rick held open a wallet containing a gold badge and ID.

"You are correct, Agent Emmett Cane. What I don't understand, is you are serving with the Federal Division of Unidentified Intelligence. Care to explain?"

"So, you believe it, right?"

Palmer shrugged. "It checks out. I've never heard of you before, but it's there. I would never have known you people existed had you not visited my little town."

Cane removed a black box from the bag. He held it out so Palmer could see the touch screen. "Alright. You see this? It's a tracking device. Damn thing has run out of charge, but I traced your comet to the woodland on the outskirts. The Federal Division of Unidentified Intelligence, or FDUI, is exactly what it says it is. We monitor signs of intelligence from sources we can't verify."

Palmer grimaced. "So, what are you talking about? Lehman's terms, please."

Cane lowered his head. A sinister expression crossed his face. "Intelligence, from beings or areas that we cannot account for. Come on, Sheriff, you know what I mean." He paused. "We're the real life X Files."

Palmer sighed. "X Files, you say? Are you referring to aliens?"

Cane sat in the chair once more. "The reality is, we just don't know. Our radio waves are full of messages and conversations. They go around the world, twenty four seven. Billions of transcripts on various different frequencies circle the planet, but sometimes, some things we find just don't make sense. It may be a language that we can't understand, or a code we struggle to decipher. Where there is a sign of intelligence that no one can understand, or are unable to trace, we come in."

"So, you're telling me that our government established your division to search for aliens? Is that correct?"

Cane shook his head. "No. Our biggest concern is the possible threat posed by the Soviets. Our government grew concerned that these signals may hold encrypted information that posed a threat to our security. Back in the sixties, a field agent witnessed some kind of event in Nevada. His testimony, and that of the division he worked with, prompted the government to create the FDUI, and ensure we are aware of anything that cannot be explained. It's our job to remain one step ahead, at all times."

"The event. What was it?"

"With the agent?"

Palmer nodded.

"We don't know. It's always been a highly classified case. Actually, that agent was the division leader until he retired, some fifteen years ago now."

Palmer shuffled in the chair. "So, say that I believe you. Can you explain these strange night lights we are having, and the comet that fell in to the woods?"

"During our investigations we discovered some kind of intelligence that wasn't traced to our enemies, so to speak. Now, the phenomena like you are experiencing is new, but not unique. There's various cases throughout history where similar instances have occurred. The most famous being the Mary Celeste and the Bermuda Triangle."

Palmer frowned. "They're famous because everyone involved vanished."

"They are, and therein lies the problem. We have access to the secret files and cases that the people of this country have no idea exist. The President's little, black book. Inside that book are the particulars about these cases. I have to report my findings of this journey back to the division, but I'll tell you this now; this town is not safe."

"From what?"

"The comet. It wasn't a comet that fell in to the woodland. It was a form of transport."

"What the hell are you talking about?" Palmer snapped. "There was nothing found during the investigation of the area."

"Sheriff, we're dealing with technology we cannot even comprehend, here. The capsule, it's like a small pole, and is usually placed inside a shell. You didn't see the shell because it burned away in a temperature so hot it set the woodland on fire. As soon as that capsule touches down it releases whatever is inside and burns away. That way it ensures nothing can be messed with. You have to trust me on this one. If you don't do something soon, and I mean within the next twenty four hours or so, there will be hell to pay."

Palmer sighed. "Cane, I believe you served, or are actively serving somewhere as a civil servant, but I'm not buying this at all. I think the stress of the job has got to you." He stood up.

"No, wait! It's the truth!"

"I'll send someone to escort you down to the cells. Maybe then you'll want to talk."

"Sheriff! No!"

Palmer left the room, ensuring to secure the door. He stood a moment, listening to Cane's muffled protests. The crafty A - hole almost had him. He almost believed.

## 23

The open country was a hell of a lot cooler than The Fall. It became clear to Tad that he should have planned this. The track expelled mud and water across his trousers, as his bike navigated its terrain, cooling him even more. The trees remained silent, but the fog fell thicker out her for sure. Visibility looked to be two, maybe three feet ahead. A red light flickered from the tree line as he approached. Tad slowed and dismounted the cycle, dragging it from the road in to the shrubbery. Damn, it was cold. It felt like walking in to an open freezer. Tad approached the light, his feet rustling the vegetation. The light flickered. It looked about to die.

"Oh shit!" he whispered. Billy's bike lay on its side. The red light he'd followed had been from its rear, flickering as the batteries gave out their last burst of energy. Fear washed over him. Billy was in danger.

"You lost out here, young man?" Tad span around. "Or just curious?"

Mister McCallum glared back, his body illuminated by the lamp in hand.

"No, sir, I…."

"What's this you've found?"

Tad backed away. "Nothing, I, don't think."

"Well, I don't believe so." McAllum wandered to Billy's bike and squatted at its side. "Did someone come here with you?"

Tad shook his head. The fear inside his veins surged unlike anything he'd ever felt. "No. I'm on my own. I found it."

McCallum rose to his feet and wandered across to Tad. "You must be honest with me. Are you on your own?" Tad trembled. McCallum held the lamp at eye level, illuminating his face against a backdrop of grey cloud. "You have nothing to fear, but you must be honest, boy. Does this belong to a friend of yours?"

Tad nodded. "Yes, but we didn't come here together. He came up last night, at least that's what-"

"Shh, shh. Take your time." Tad's nervousness was no longer hidden. McCallum, although huge and menacing in stature, appeared likeable. His demeanour began to quell the nervousness inside. Tad became more at ease. "Now, sir, tell me. How long has your friend been here?"

"I don't know? I thought maybe since last night. That's why I came here."

"Okay. We need to find him. He may be in great danger."

"Like, how?"

McCallum looked in to the sky. His wild eyes scoured the impenetrable fog. "He just is. What's his name?"

"Billy."

McCallum wandered in to the trees, his footfalls rustling the bracken beneath. Tad had followed his glare upwards toward the hidden sky. Maybe the comet and the summer haze were connected somehow?

"Hey!" Tad turned to see the dark beard looking across its owners shoulder. "Come with me. It's not safe out here by yourself." A flicker of doubt entered his mind. What would happen if he accompanied this brute? "I also need your help to find your friend."

Tad sensed something wrong. Not with this lamp carrying behemoth, but the atmosphere itself. He knew he shouldn't have ventured out. He should have just gone home and spent the day playing Mass Effect and watching Star Wars. In reality, though, he stood in an oppressive environment with a man he didn't know, but who belonged to a cult that The Fall accused of kidnap. Maybe Billy was lost, or maybe he'd been kidnapped? One thing was certain, he was in danger.

Tad trudged through the woodland, joining McCallum in the lamp light. He sensed the man as good as his word, but prayed it was in fact true.

134

McCallum placed a hand on his shoulder. "Stay close."

The temperature dropped with every step away from the road. Tad shuddered as the fog embraced him within its freezing grasp.

"Billy?" McCallum's voice boomed through the cloud.

"Billy?" Tad replied, cupping his hands around his mouth.

They rustled and waded their way through ferns and branches, led by a light that illuminated the fallen cloud orange. Soon, they stumbled in to a small clearing.

McCallum sighed, resting the lamp on the damp leaves. He wandered back and forth, hands upon his hips. "Wait here," he ordered, reaching down to grasp the lamp once more. "There's only one other place I can think he may have found, if he's up here still."

"Where's that?"

McCallum looked to Tad. "A cluster of trees just through there. You must wait here. Do not follow me."

McCallum wandered out in to the fog, his hulking frame consumed until out of sight. Tad stood there, arms wrapped about him to stay warm, and never felt as vulnerable as he did at this moment. Even though the fog engulfed the trees, its barrier was only one of vision. Anyone could shamble from its grip, and from any direction. He felt certain his new friend was not the only weirdo lurking the woods, and with fog this thick, knew how open to attack from any angle he could be.

The more Tad stood there, the more nervous he became. How long had the guy been gone now? Two minutes? Three? What if he'd been left here on purpose, left as prey for the cult?

"Shut up, man," he whispered, bringing reality back to the situation. Nervousness took its toll, and against the weirdo's warning, Tad took a step in the direction he had vanished. Each footfall rumbled like an earthquake as he wandered in to the fog, searching for his new companion. Leaves and branches glided from the element as he ambled past, uncertain if the path he walked was correct. The urge to shout out quelled inside his body. As much as he wanted it, Tad feared a response. The chill along his back replicated the temperature. Tad grasped his arms about his body so tight they ached. His teeth chattered by themselves. Mucus tickled the end of his nose. If he didn't know any better, he'd swear it was winter. An object appeared in his path. Tad stopped, looking down. A solitary sneaker rested on the bracken. He went to squat, but the stinging cold within his body suggested otherwise. Tad studied the sole and the design. Black material, silver mesh and white laces. He gasped.

"Billy?"

Explosions of light seared through the fog. Tad stumbled, squinting against its power. Energy pulsed throughout the atmosphere, pounding inside his chest one beat at a time. The ground quaked. He fell to the damp floor, squirming himself away from the aura. Groans bellowed from the fog, like incantations from a mythical beast. Tad screamed, inaudible against the moans. Urine spread throughout his trousers.

Nothing.

A blast of light. Tad looked up, eyes filled with cloud. Three distorted shadows appeared, each looking down. He screamed. He cried out for Mom.

***

"Hey! Hey! He's coming to!"

Tad opened his eyes. The bearded face of Mister McCallum filled his vision.

"Take it easy, my young friend." Mitchum Hoyt held a lamp beyond his shoulder. "How we found you out here in this is a miracle, son, a bona-fide miracle."

# 24

Sam shared a booth with Lance as they took in their drinks. He wasn't usually a hot drinks person, but the fog had chilled his core. A steaming mug of coffee perched upon the table separating them both. Looking around, only a family sat at the opposite end, within a booth similar to theirs. A whole counter of empty stools and chequered flooring separated them.

"You're asking me to do something real bad, Sam."

Sam rolled his eyes. "For God's sake, Lance. I'll do it myself."

Lance leant across the table, lowering his voice. "What has he done that's got you so wound up?"

"He just exists."

"Geez. And you're prepared to ruin his life? I mean, damn, man. He's your brother."

"Not mine," Sam snapped. "That little bastard is the apple of my Mom's eye. It makes me sick. I don't blame Dad for being out there, screwing around with other women. This family sucks."

"You do know that a beating like what you're talking about would cripple him, or give him brain damage, or something."

Sam sipped his coffee. "That's the whole purpose."

Lance screwed his face. "Sam; I'll throw my weight around if I need to. I may even be called a bully, but there's no way I'll take part in something like this. You could kill him, you know that?"

Sam shook his head. "You know, I have a mother at home. Listen to you, preaching like your some kind of golden boy. You've messed people up. You've got a record. What makes you too good to do this?"

Lance sat back on the red upholstery. "The fact that I'm not crazy. You're right about one thing, though; I do have a record. I haven't been the best of people and I'll admit it. But what you're asking? Man, you need help. Who do you want to piss off the most?

137

Tad or your Mom? To me, it sounds like there's something underlying with you, something that's making your brain misfire."

Sam's agitation festered in to anger. His nostrils flared. "You calling me crazy?" he growled.

Lance stood from the table. "Yeah. Yeah I am. I don't want anything to do with this. And, I don't want anything more to do with you. You're beyond help. Keep the hell away from me."

Lance walked out, no parting words, no nothing. Sam sighed, placing the mug back on the table. 'Tad. You rat bastard. You've now cost me my best friend. Is there anything in my life you won't screw up?'

## 25

Tad sat in a dusty old room. Flames roared within the confines of a dilapidated fire place. He remembered the shadows, but only just. Was it a dream? It felt like that. That memory seemed so real. So far away, but so real. He pulled the blanket McCallum had given around his shoulders, picked up the china mug that held tea and took a sip. Something scared him. It wasn't McCallum, Mitchum Hoyt or his surrounding, but something deeper.

The old door creaked as Mitchum Hoyt entered. Tad glanced his way.

"Tad!"

Tad gasped. "Billy?"

Billy ran across the exposed floorboards, his hefty frame compressing them underfoot. "What the hell are you doing here?"

Tad slumped back. Overcome with emotion, he began to whimper. "What is it? What's happening around here? What happened to me?"

Hoyt strolled across to the old sofa by the fire and took a seat. He leaned across and held Tad by the shoulder.

"Young man, whatever happens from now on, you must understand you are in no danger." The fedora rested once more on his head. He didn't look evil, at least not how the town-folk described. McCallum left the leader in the company of their young guests.

Tad wiped a tear from his cheek. "Mister Hoyt, sir? What happened?"

"Son, that's not for me to say. It's a story for another day, but trust me, that day will come, and soon. We found this on you." Hoyt tossed a marble to him. Tad took it between his thumb and index finger. Through watery eyes he studied the sphere made of glass. Inside, a blue cloud drifted within the confines, bouncing against its barrier and dispersing in an alternate direction.

Tad's fear turned to intrigue. "What is it?"

"That, my friend, is proof that you are pure of heart. You will walk freely upon the Earth when all is done."

"I don't get it," Billy replied.

Hoyt laughed, leaned forward once more and clasped his hands. "Can you not feel the aura your friend omits?"

Come to think of it, there was a strange feel to the place. Tad no longer felt afraid, he felt at ease. Something felt different, something inside him. He'd gone from afraid to confident in a matter of seconds.

"Rest assured, my young friend, you have nothing left to fear. Keep that close to you. You've been through a passage of rite, and you may never know how important its sentiment will be to you."

Tad glanced to Hoyt. "What, like a trial or something?"

Hoyt nodded. "Kind of. That dream you had? It wasn't a dream."

A shudder passed over his body. "You mean, I was actually there?"

"They aren't the pleasantest of creatures, that's for damn sure," Hoyt began, "but, they saw something in you that felt familiar. They'll protect you now until the end of your days."

Whether it was the day's events playing havoc on his mind or not, Tad just couldn't understand.

"Are they the ones that took those police officers, and those people living on Glenn Avenue?" Billy turned on the floor and crossed his legs.

Hoyt nodded. "Some will come back, and some won't."

"Wait, wait, wait." Tad shuffled around to face Hoyt. "How do you know?"

"Yeah. How do you know so much about them?" Billy gazed upon Hoyt. Tad noticed how mesmerised his friend appeared by their storyteller.

Hoyt smiled. "I don't. I only know what I have to."

"But who are they?" Tad placed his drink down.

"Like I said, that's a story for another day. Come on, Mister McCallum will run you back."

He stood, and gestured for the boys to do the same.

"Do you know what really happened to those boys from school that went missing, Mister Hoyt?" Hoyt stopped. The atmosphere dropped to oppression. Tad regretted his question.

Hoyt's head turned. "They are gone." His voice was cold and blunt. "Now, get your belongings. You must be home before dark."

Altman and Miss Olivia rode in the back of the Chevrolet with the boys' pushbikes, allowing Tad and Billy the comfort of a closed cab. Mister McAllum drove with caution. The fog, much more dense than it had been, was now treacherous.

"What we're you doing up here?" Tad asked his friend as they swayed with the road.

"I came up to see what was going on but got lost in the fog. It was so cold I thought I would freeze my butt off."

"When was that?"

"My watch read five when I first looked."

"Holy cow, Billy. How'd you last that long?"

Billy smiled, pinching his winter coat. "I've never been so happy to wear a coat. Even when I sat down to rest, I was warm. I must have dozed off or something, but when I woke, one of these people stood over me. Man, I shat my pants. I think I actually did a little piss."

Tad looked across to McCallum, and couldn't say whether he smiled. McCallum was a hulking, intimidating figure, even sat behind the wheel. Tad looked to his clouded marble. He felt strange. The marble had a similar effect to him as the One Ring. He knew to keep it with him always, and planned on doing so.

From the distance two red lights appeared in the fog. Altman banged the roof from the rear as the vehicle slowed.

"Get out," McCallum ordered. Tad met his stare. "Now!"

Billy fumbled at the door. Lights appeared in the fog. Two men with flashlights approached.

"Hey? Hey! What are you doing there!"

The door opened. Frozen air surged inside. From the fog appeared the resident hunters, Buck Jeffley and Terry Logan, both looming from the cloud. Tad sensed something wrong. Buck approached, dressed in his usual red and black chequered shirt and jeans. Curly hair protruded from beneath a cap. Logan looked a few years younger than he did, clad in his green shirt and camo trousers.

"I said what are you doing there, assholes?"

It was too late. There was no way Tad and Billy could escape without alerting them.

McCallum opened his door. "Is there some kind of problem I can help you with?" he asked, dwarfing the cab from which he emerged.

Buck smiled. "Well, well. If it isn't Miller Falls resident sasquatch. I asked what the hell it is you're doing here?"

"It's a road." Altman jumped down from the Chevy and stood beside his brethren. "What does it look like we're doing?"

The hunters chuckled, illuminated by the vehicle headlights. "Seems we got ourselves a little bit of an attitude, don't it, T?"

"Sure does," Terry replied.

"What do we do?" Billy whispered as both boys watched from the cab.

"I got no idea, but it looks like shit's going down!" Tad grasped the marble within his fist. Both the hunters carried rifles.

"I'm gonna ask you again, you inbred, hillbilly douchebags. What are you doing?" Buck's smile deteriorated.

*'This is bad. This is real, real, bad!'* Tad thought as the atmosphere dropped. The hunter's passed close to the vehicle bonnet. In a single moment, Buck's eyes found Tad.

"What the hell is this?" He turned to McAllum. The rifle raised.

"Go!" McAllum screamed.

Tad ploughed out of the cab and fell to the road.

"Shit!"

Tad pushed up, helped by Billy. "Hey! Get here!"

"Go!"

Miss Olivia pushed the boys from the vehicle.

"No!"

Tad jumped as the sound of gunfire echoed through the fog. Dead weight fell upon him.

"Tad!"

He turned to find Billy supporting the woman aiding their escape. She'd used him to support herself. Her eyes filled with fear.

"Go," she whispered. Olivia fell heavy against them. "Go."

Unable to take the burden, Tad released her to the ground. A bullet hole appeared in her clothing, decorated with a vibrant, red splash.

"Olivia!" Altman boomed.

"Shit!" Terry whispered.

Yanked by his collar, Tad lost his footing. "Move!" Billy screamed.

"Get back here!"

But they didn't. Tad sprinted beside Billy, past the hunters and in to the fog. His legs pumped as fast as he had ever pushed them.

"Get back here!"

But they we're gone, lost to the element in which they ran. Gunfire echoed from behind. Billy lagged back.

"Come on!"

They sprinted along the road, the cold air attacking them from all directions. The sound of an engine fired from behind.

"Come on, Bill!"

The burn of exhaustion engulfed Tad's chest. A vehicle appeared ahead of them. The tyres screeched as it halted, only centimetres away. Officers Duggan and York stepped out.

"They shot her!" Tad screamed.

"What? Calm down!" Michael drew his gun. An engine roared through the fog.

"Get back!" Alex shouted, pushing Billy past their car. The headlights appeared as Buck's truck bound closer.

"Get back!" Michael pushed Tad off of the road as the truck ploughed in to the police car. Glass and plastic shattered, searing in to the air. Metal buckled as the bonnets smashed. The siren whirred and jarred as the car span across the tarmac. Tad thumped to the floor, his breath expelling in plumes. Time stood still for that moment. He lay looking upward, to a cloud in which he was engulfed.

"Get out of the car! Get out!" Michael had reacted and taken control. Tad sat upright, watching as the police officer dragged Buck from the driver's seat. Tad slumped back, catching his breath. What now?

\*\*\*

Palmer power marched through the station, his anger increasing with each step. He'd dispatched Alex and Michael to run in Hoyt again, and just at the right time. The Feds were out of town, probably resting up in some luxury accommodation at tax payer's expense. Brooks was at home, having covered the morning shift for him. Today of all days, this had to happen. With only Officer Diana Trent to add to the mix, he'd had to pull Duggan and York from the beat to sit with the good old boys, Millers Fall resident idiots, Buck Jeffley and Terry Logan, each isolated in the holding cells until called for interrogation.

He'd had the story from his officer's already. The boy's accounts, their statements, even the fact that Hoyt had seized the body within minutes of the shooting, taking advantage of the officers whilst they were tied up with the hunters. With everything else happening in this damn town, he now had to deal with a murder. He hadn't made it anywhere near the cells when Jeanette's voice caught his attention.

"Sheriff? Sheriff!"

"What?" He turned to face her.

"Sheriff! Outside! Out front! It's Hoyt!"

144

His stomach dropped. "Get Alex, Michael and Diana! Now!" Palmer sprinted through the corridor, grasping his holster. Jeanette passed him. "Quickly!"

He raced across the reception area and out through the external door.

The fog settled on the green across the way. About them it drifted, eerie and graceful. Mitchum Hoyt stoop upon the steps, his head lowered, peering to the lifeless body of Miss Olivia. Palmer stopped and found the eyes of Hoyt's followers. They surrounded the station entrance, from the road to the steps. The Chevy hummed within an otherwise silence as the denim clad, backwoods people peered back.

"She was a good girl, Sheriff. Never put a foot wrong. Wouldn't hurt a fly. A true lover of nature." Hoyt smiled beneath the Fedora. "A true lover of life." Hoyt's gaze met Palmer. His beard lifted in amusement. "Look about you." Hoyt's arms rose, as though seeking praise. "Look at my people. Do we look like the threatening type, to you?" Palmer remained silent. "Do we!" Hoyt bellowed, his expression now one of anguish. "We have lived in peace, away from you! Away from your society! Away from this cursed life in which you lead! We have never, *never* given you reason to walk our ground! We have never requested anything from you, yet still we are blamed! We are the cause of this town's problems! We are the ones who bring about the problems of Millers Fall!" Hoyt's arms dropped. He stood, a man dejected. "Sheriff, we are simple people living a simple life, and because of the prejudice of this town we have paid for it."

"Shit!" Michael and Alex burst in to the fog. Diana emerged, her gun drawn.

Palmer span around, palm outward. He needn't say anything. They would know to back down.

"Mister Hoyt, you have my deepest sympathies," Palmer began, addressing the cult leader, "and I will ensure justice is served. You have my word."

145

"Oh, I'm sure you will. In fact, I have no doubt. What I want to know is how you deal with this society?" Hoyt beckoned to the crowd. Mister McAllum, Altman and the giant hidden by burlap sack waded through the bodies.

"This is not good, Sheriff," Michael whispered.

"Stand strong, guys."

"Sheriff, I'd like to introduce you to Isaac." Isaac stood as tall as Mister McAllum, if not taller. His shirt was tight and torn, revealing a body sculptured of hard work on the farm. The burlap sack concealing his features tied with string around his neck. Hoyt slapped the giant between the shoulders. "Isaac found me some years ago." Hoyt's hands found his trouser pockets as he wandered up and down in front of the officers. Against the fog and group of henchmen, he appeared a threat. "Spurned by society for looking different. Because he was not accepted. In fact, Isaac was ridiculed by those who perceived themselves better than he. They we're wrong! Isaac is a person embracing life, enjoying life, living free with less than a care of what the world thinks of him." Hoyt stopped. "At least, he was. Until this." He gestured to the body at his feet. "Now he seeks vengeance."

"Hoyt, that will not be necessary." Palmer sensed the beginning of a conflict. "We have statements. We have witnesses. Justice will be served, for you, your people, and the deceased."

Hoyt chuckled. "Sheriff? I'm just not sure that's enough, anymore." He cocked his head, peering from the corner of his eyes. "I've held on to the thought that somewhere in your world, there is a decency within society. It kept me motivated, kept me going, striving to prove myself right. Unfortunately, tonight that notion was dashed. An innocent, un-armed woman has been killed at the hands of your own people, no less. And you know what she was doing?" He sneered to the officers. "She was returning those two boys to the town, to make sure they returned home safe."

A deep, animalistic grunt emerged within the tension. Palmer turned to Isaac. The hulk dropped to his knees, sobbing as he leaned across the body. The burlap sack trembled with his movements.

"It's okay, my friend. It's okay." Hoyt wandered across, placing a hand atop the sack.

"Mister Hoyt, may I suggest you and your people return to your property. There's nothing more you can do here." Palmer knew he'd have to be strong. Any weakness in his persona could create a riot. He spoke confident and to the point. Just get them all moving on and avoid confrontation.

Isaac stood, assisted by Hoyt. "You're right, Sheriff. You're absolutely right. Know this, though. We will not protect you anymore. You've made the decision, and we will abide. We will return to our home and pray for Miss Olivia, as that is all we can do. Come, now, back to the vehicles." Hoyt gestured for McAllum and Altman to assist Isaac.

Palmer sighed. The plethora of dirty bodies, rustic colours and unkempt hair dispersed, and without incident.

"Sheriff. One more thing." Hoyt looked to him as the vehicles loaded. "Notice anything different, tonight? Anything at all?" Palmer frowned. Hoyt's features twisted. His smile teased. The leader flicked his head. "Check your watch." Palmer looked to his wrist. 0003.

"What?"

Hoyt chuckled. "Maybe that strange, sunset you've been so accustomed to at this late hour is too familiar for you to recognise?"

"Shit," Alex whispered. "The sunset."

Hoyt chucked. Malevolence crossed his face. Staring directly back to Palmer he spoke. "They're here."

# 26

Tad sat atop his bed. He should've been sleeping, but the night's events whirled around within his mind. Fog, hillbillies, hunters, shootings, death. Mom had been to collect him. He was grounded again, this time forever. She'd spent the last few hours with her old friend the bottle. He just couldn't switch off. The marble received from Hoyt sat upon the bedside desk. It was strange. The sense of confidence it gave felt immense. Out of the window the fog rolled, hiding all but the closest items. Mister Jenner next door must still been awake. A dim light shone where a window used to stand.

Dad had to stop in a motel out on the route to Port Sandown. The weather had diminished so bad that no vehicles were heading in or out of town. That's what Buck and Terry had been doing. Parked on the road, swigging beer, shooting their weapons off and not thinking about the consequences. Look what happened there.

From the darkness a dull, blue light appeared against the bedroom walls. Tad turned, knowing his electronics shut down for the night. "No way," he whispered. The marble pulsed. Inquisitive, Tad moved to the desk, grasping the marble between his fingers. The dark cloud swirled inside, illuminated by a vibrant, blue light. "What the hell?"

A gentle knock rattled his door. Tad hid the marble in a duvet fold. "Come in," he whispered. Then, he wished he hadn't. Sam entered, turned and locked the door. Tad moved across his bed.

"Sam. Sam, I-"

"Shhh," he whispered, walking across the room. His knuckles clicked. "Tad, you're really starting to piss me off." Within the darkness Sam's glare looked cold. "Doesn't matter what happens, it seems I'm always the one suffering."

"Sam, it's your own damn fault." Tad felt a beating coming, so didn't hold back. "If you weren't such a dick, you wouldn't get treated the way you do."

Sam smiled. "Part of me wants to believe that, Tad. Honestly, it does. Problem is, I've contributed more to this family than you, and I'm still not accepted."

"Like what? What have you ever done to help out Mom and Dad?"

Sam leant closer. "I've kept this family together. You know Dad? You know he's screwing around with other women don't you?"

"What?"

"Oh yeah. He's been doing it for years. I've caught him on more than one occasion. And, he knows that I know."

"You gonna tell Mom?"

"Nah, I get more bargaining power like this. I think she knows, anyway. Otherwise she wouldn't be so drunk that she's passed out in their bedroom." Sam patted Tad on the shoulder. "She won't come. Not this time."

Tad dashed for the door, but his pyjama top snagged and he fell back. The first punch blasted his sternum. Tad crumpled, his stomach aching as he dropped. The second smashed like a sledgehammer. An image appeared within his mind. Tad stood on a rail track, in a crisp, autumn day. The breeze cooled his skin as it fluttered past. A locomotive approached. Unable to move, he cried out. The train struck.

Tad fell back on to his bed. Sam towered above, his knuckles glistening in the blue light. Something rested in his mouth. He flopped to one side, allowing the item to escape. A tooth fell on to the duvet.

Sam smirked. "That happened when you fell off your bike, didn't it?"

All throughout his being, Tad hurt. His nose tingled and eyes streamed. The blunt pain cascading between his ribs became unbearable. This was as harsh a beating as he had taken. The taste of metal flooded his mouth.

"Get lost, Sam. I'm telling this time, no matter what. I'll have the face to prove it. You'll have to kill me."

His head jarred in to the mattress. A fist smashed against his cheek. Shit, that really hurt.

"That's fine, little brother. I can play this game all night. Dad's screwing his girlfriend in the next town and Mom's passed out in the other room. Ain't no-one coming to help you."

A light flickered against his wall. Sam stopped, looking up on to the ceiling. The blue light pulsed, now dark in colour, but somehow bright. Its aura intensified with each wave. Tad looked across to his desk. The marble expelled shafts of light that plastered the bedroom. Its cloud burned white at the centre. The plumes swirled and swirled, intensifying within the brightness. The desk trembled. Star Wars models shook on their stands. Books edged from their shelves. Sam lost his balance. "Earthquake!" he shouted, staying upright.

Tad sighed. The confidence came back to him. Somehow he knew this would be the end of it. Through the aches and pain, he smiled. The burden of torment lifted. "No, not this time," he replied.

A surge of power snapped throughout the bedroom. The light streamed in to wondrous, white lightning, thrashing around as it exploded from the sphere. Wind gusted from the light, ruffling their hair and clothing.

Sam circled, inspecting the bolts. "What? What's happening?"

Strands of light snapped, coiling around both wrists. He struggled. "Hey? Hey!" Sam cried, straining to break free. "Tad!" Sam's eyes exuded fear. Tad continued his smile. "Tad! Come on!" Tad shook his head and flipped the bird. "Tad!"

Lightning passed across Sam's abdomen. He screamed. In its wake, shredded clothes and blood appeared. "Shit, Tad! Shit!" Sam screamed. "Oh God!" The lightning grasped its catch, turning it to face the light. Blood cascaded across his trousers. From the bright aura, a shaded figure emerged. It was undefined, standing against the light, but humanoid. The figure reached down, investigation Sam's injury. Tad watched as it placed a hand inside his brother. Sam screamed, flailing his limbs. The scream, so guttural, so terrifying, brought goosebumps to Tad's back. The figure reeled out Sam's intestine, like a firehouse unravelling from its coil. Sam cried, throwing his head back and forth. "Ah, God! Ah, shit! Ah, my God!" The innards slopped to the carpet as the figure continued. With the other hand it entered Sam's quaking body, removing anything and everything it could. Tad watched as dark lumps fell on top of the colon, his liver, kidneys, everything, feeling no remorse. Sam screamed, his pitch higher than a schoolgirl. The wind rushed to the figure. Open books rattled, papers flapped. The light burned. Chaos erupted. Models crashed from their resting place. Shelves fell from the walls. The breeze thundered inside his ears. It stopped. The room fell silent. It fell dark.

Tad perched on the end of his bed. His body, aching from the beat down, now embraced the sense of calm within the room. The Millennium Falcon hung from the ceiling, one of a few not smashed upon the floor. The shelves sat where they always had, on his walls and full of books. He looked toward the desk. No guts or internal organs lay upon his carpet. Not even a drop of blood rest there. He sat, attempting to make sense of it. Was it a dream? No, it couldn't be, his body throbbed from Sam's fists. It had to have happened.

Tad stood, walking across to his bedroom door. It opened with little more than a squeak. He peered out in to the corridor, first right toward the stairs, then left, toward Sam's room. The empty hall stood silent. The only noise drawing attention was the clock downstairs, ticking away to an empty room, as though nothing had happened. The house only fell this quiet in the dead of night. The bedroom remained stable. The Mass Effect clock displayed the time at a little after four.

"No way," he whispered, clutching the rib that still ached. Ever inquisitive, Tad moved in to the corridor, walking on his tiptoes as children do when they don't want to be caught. He thought about knocking Sam's door, but found it open and took that as an invitation. The hallway light flooded in to the room. A Millers Fall banner stood proud above his bed. Well, Sam was the star quarterback, after all. It's a shame only their parents knew how much of a dick he was. Some good girly posters on display, too. Chasey Lain, if he wasn't mistaken. They looked dated, but hey, he'd have them. Guess Mom didn't come in here very often. Tad returned his attention to the bed. It was made, which shocked him a little. Tad couldn't imagine Sam having time to, or even be bothered to make a bed. It lay empty, though, which meant Sam wasn't residing in there.

"Sam?" he whispered, not knowing what to expect. The room remained silent. Remembering Sam's temperament, Tad took a step back, just in case the jerk flew from a hiding place. "Sam?" he asked again, peering from the doorframe in to the gloom. Still nothing. Only Chasey's eyes and provocative expression seemed to reply.

Tad shuffled down the hall to their parent's room. Opening the door, he found their Mom on her side, facing away from him. "Mom?" he said, wincing as his asked. She stirred, rolling within the duvet. "Mom?"

She turned, opening her eyes in a semi-conscious state. "What is it, honey?"

"I don't know where Sam is."

"What?"

"He's not in his room, and I can't hear him downstairs."

She sighed, resting her head back on the pillow. "I bet he's stayed out again, like I asked him not to." She looked to him, now more aware. "Don't worry about it. Your brother will often stay out until daybreak. It's just something he does. Go back to bed, he'll be back in the morning." She smiled. Tad nodded and closed the door.

He stood looking out of his window in to the fog. God knows how, but it was raining, too. Millers Fall was in the grip of some seriously messed up weather. What happened to Sam felt like a dream. Perhaps that was why it felt so easy to accept. Still, the missing tooth and bruises he'd found whilst in the bathroom taking a piss not five minutes ago proved that something had happened.

The fog was boring, now. Tad fell back on his bed, forgetting his injuries for a moment and yelped out. He'd lost about three hours of the night, and his brother, too. Something weird was happening. He rolled on to his side, facing the desk. The marble caught his attention. No longer did it swirl with dark, inky clouds. Tiny pulses of lightning flickered inside, within a swirling, red mass.

## 27

"Okay, gather round." Sheriff Palmer beckoned to his work-force. Michael, Alex, Diana, Deputy Brooks and Jeanette came to his office entrance. Palmer slumped against the frame, folding his arms. "Listen, I just got off the phone with Sergeant Harris up at the hospital." He sighed, rubbing a palm across his face. Bristles rustled against his hand. "Finn didn't make it."

"What?" Michael sighed.

"Oh no," Jeanette whimpered.

"He passed away about fifteen minutes ago. His family was there with him."

The atmosphere hung about him like a lead necklace. Diana sobbed. Alex placed his arm around her.

"They know what it was?" Michael asked.

"They won't know fully until the coroner's report comes in. He underwent hours of surgery, but every time they fixed something up they found something else." Palmer looked away. Emotion crept to the back of his eyes. Whether it was Finn or the situation, he was unsure. "Anyway, we're on our own now until the fog clears. Outside the town there is zero visibility. Our colleagues are stuck, the Feds are stuck. There's no way anyone can get in or out. Let's just hope it keeps Hoyt on his farm and the townspeople in their homes. I'll call the radio station, ask them to read a bulletin advising people to stay inside."

"Do we know how long it's gonna last?" Alex asked.

Palmer shrugged. "No idea. According to the MET office, it shouldn't even be here. Okay, go have a coffee or something, get your heads together. I'm gonna speak with Anthony and plan what we do next."

"Is there even anything we can do, next?" Michael asked.

"Best thing to do is show our presence to the people of The Fall. You and Alex take a vehicle, just patrol around, show everyone we're still here. Take it easy, though, the last thing I need is for you both to vanish out there."

As everyone moved, beginning their tasks, Palmer turned to Jeanette. "Listen, you may as well go home. There's nothing really you can do here. I'd rather know that you're safe than have you here."

"Is there nothing I can do?" she asked.

He shook his head. "Admin can wait. Just get yourself back, rested and ready to begin tomorrow."

"Only if you're sure?"

He smiled. "I'm sure. Go. Have a rest."

It was clear she wasn't happy with his request, but in time she'd thank him for doing it.

# 28

Tad didn't hang around that morning. The urge to wander outside became too great. Mom was still asleep, he'd checked before leaving. Dad was gone, and Sam was missing. The bruises had emerged during his sleep, making him look like he'd gone ten rounds with Brock Lesnar.

He reached in to his pocket and produced the marble. It continued with its inky, red swirls. Tad smiled a fresh, toothless grin. *'I wonder if you're trapped in there?'*

Tad's demeanour changed. He chose black jeans, black tee shirt and a black hoodie to repel the cold fog he was about to embrace. Black had always been worn with other colours, never before in entirety by itself. Wild, unkempt hair obscured his vision. He pulled the hood across to reduce the wind chill. Stepping outside, he reached the cell phone from his pocket.

"Billy, talk to me."

"What is it, Tad? You sound, well, different. You okay?"

"To be honest, I'm not sure. I don't know what I'm feeling. I don't know what I'm doing. I just... I think I'm leaving. The Fall. Running away. But I'm gonna wander the streets. Something is wrong with me."

"What are you talking about? Listen, come over to my house. Play Xbox..."

"No. No, Billy. Just...thanks, but I gotta be on my own."

"Tad, I don't think you're well. Okay, well I'll come to you-"

"No!" Tad snapped, "That's a real bad idea."

"What? Why?"

"I don't know. I just...I have a feeling. Something terrible will happen."

"Now you're getting scary."

"Billy, this is it. I'm going. Thank you, for being my friend. Tell Jake I said goodbye."

"What? Hey, wait…."

Tad pressed the screen and ended the call. He dropped the phone to the sidewalk and smashed it with his heel. The screen crackled beneath the repetitive strikes, until nothing more than circuit boards and shattered plastic littered the area. Finally, reaching down, Tad grabbed what was once his most treasured belonging and threw it in to the fog. He had no idea why, or what spurred him to do it, but something nestled in the back of his mind confirmed that this was the last act from the old Tad. Now it started afresh. The story of his life was about to commence. That journey began somewhere else within The Fall.

Something called….

## 29

"What kind of country-ass, screw up of a town do we live in?" Michael asked, peering through the window as they passed through the fallen cloud. "We have fog, we have rain, we have fog-rain. You think they have fog-rain in San Francisco, LA or New York?"

Alex chuckled. "What the hell is fog-rain?"

Michael flapped at the weather outside. "This. This is fog-rain. Look at it."

"This is rain in the fog. Technically, fog-rain would be rain that rained fog, not water."

Michael sighed, slumping back in the seat. He watched the shadows of buildings pass by, grey, dark, and eerie within the cloud.

They passed along Tanners Avenue, through King Street and on to Main Street.

As they crawled across the tarmac, a thought occurred to him.

"Alex. There's nobody out here."

"What?" Alex smirked back.

Michael pushed himself up within the seat. "Seriously. Look. How many people have you seen out here since we've been patrolling, huh? Cars? Pedestrians?"

"Maybe because there's an unofficial curfew? That night the woods caught fire we didn't see people. Add to that the advice for everyone to stay indoors and off the street, and I'd say you have your answer."

"No, I just have this feeling it's something else." Michael grimaced. "It doesn't feel empty. It doesn't even feel sleepy, like everyone is hiding away keeping themselves to themselves. It just feels…. it feels dead out there."

Denny's Store loomed ahead. "Well, we're in the shopping district now. If we're going to see anyone, it will be around here someplace."

Michael lost his trail of thought and cracked a laugh. "Shopping district? In Millers Fall? Would that be anywhere near the financial sector or does it stand alone?"

"No, listen, you jerk. We have the shops on our right." Alex removed a hand from the steering wheel and gestured through his window, as if presenting the cluster of shops as a big deal, "and on our left, we have some residential buildings. You want to pull over and do a door to door?"

Michael began to answer, but his attention drew elsewhere in an instant. "The hell?" he asked, as the vehicle headlights revealed an object in the road.

Alex leaned closer to the wheel. "What is that?"

The vehicle stopped before a wheelchair, tipped on its side. Their headlights glinted from the metallic frame. "That has to be Jake Newsome's, no-one else in town uses one."

Michael opened his door. "What has he done?" Cold struck from every direction as he moved to the front of the car. "Jake?"

Michael turned, scouring the area for the wheelchair's owner. The rain became snow.

"Look at this." Alex held a hand out and looked up in to the cloud. "Snow."

"If something's happened to Jake out here, he'll freeze."

"Come on. Let's have a look around."

The officers followed a small path to Jake's detached home, not far opposite the store. Alex rattled the frame with three knocks. The door opened.

"Hello?" Alex asked.

"No-one there?"

They stood in silence. The breeze howled softly as it drifted by. Alex cocked his head, peering through the gap. "Jake? Hello? It's Alex. Are you okay?" He prodded the door, allowing it to open a little more. The hallway stood dark, illuminated only by the poor daylight.

Michael peered in. "There's no light, no sound or anything. I think we should investigate."

Alex stepped across the threshold, opening the door. The stairwell to the left appeared normal. The rail running along and up the wall signified the presence of a chair lift.

"Hey," Michael whispered, drawing Alex's attention. "Look, the chair is upstairs." They both observed the generic, white finished seat resting atop the landing.

A look of confusion crossed Alex's face. "Jake's wheelchair is outside. The guy can't walk. How the hell did his chair get outside if he was upstairs?" He turned to Michael, clicking the safety from his gun. "You want to go up there? I'll search down here, see what I can find."

Michael ascended the steps, taking his time as though not to disturb the house's occupant. Something felt wrong. No light, no sound, it didn't even feel like any heating had been used.

The top floor was wrecked. Papers, files, everything scattered about the floor. Wardrobes upturned in the master bedroom, clothes strewn across the floor, it appeared as if Jake had been the victim of a burglary.

Michael continued, heading to the bedroom where Jake might be. "Jake?" he asked, praying there was some kind of response. A vision popped in to his mind, finding Jake murdered on top of his mattress. "Get a grip." But just to make sure, he reached to the sidearm. The bedroom was destroyed, but empty. Jake didn't appear within these four walls. Backing away, Michael wandered back to the hall and investigated the other two rooms. One was an office of some sort, with a computer tower system and desk taking most of the area. The next room looked like a guest bedroom, with a single bed, chair and set of draws dotted around. Both had been ransacked, but not to the extent of the master room.

Michael turned his attention to the final door, opening it to reveal a wet room.

He became nauseous.

Blood splattered across the tiles and shower curtain. It trickled from the wash basin. The drain clogged with some form of solid, refusing the liquid to drain from the floor and instead allowing it to form across the surface.

Michael placed a fist across his mouth. "Holy…" he whispered, his gaze fixed on the claret formed on the floor. The drain gurgled, allowing three bubbles to escape and pop. Michael watched, his expression one of disgust, as more emerged. The drain sang a morbid chorus as air escaped and popped to the surface. The blood shifted, as though something moved below its surface. Michael drew his gun and moved closer. The blood wasn't deep, and looked like an accumulation of everything running from the walls. It exploded, splattering his face and uniform. He fell back as a claret hand lurched out, reaching to his leg. His boot smashed the appendage as he fell back, tumbling out to the hallway. Falling sideways, Michael smashed to the floor, aiming the gun and taking fire. The first shot missed. The second sliced directly through the palm as a squeal reverberated against the tiles. The third popped in to the puddle, scaring the hand to withdraw and vanish beneath the surface.

"What is it? Michael?" came Alex's voice as he ascended the stairs.

"I don't know, man! Something was in there! Something tried to grab me!"

"What happened here?"

"God-dammit, man," Michael sighed. He sat upright, gasping out. His heart pounded with a sense of urgency.

"Here." Alex handed Michael a towel that had been resting across the banister. He wiped his face, surprised to see the amount of blood he'd taken off. "Was someone here?"

"I don't know," Michael began, shaking his head. "It was something. It looked like a hand, reaching out from the blood in there."

Alex moved to the doorframe. "You think you disturbed whoever did this?" he asked, scouring the walls about him.

"It was empty when I got here. I don't know how I'd miss someone already inside."

The drain gurgled. "There's too much blood for the drain to...."

Blood exploded in to the air. Hands reached from its surface, smashing down on the floor before lurching a head and torso from its depths. A wild, high scream pierced the building. A female form reached out, her long hair matted as she writhed sideways to escape the puddle. Michael pushed up to his feet, jumping the stairs to the ground floor. He clattered in to Alex as they fell through the door and out in to the snowfall. All about them, at the edges of vision, greying forms loomed, watching the officer's retreat to their car. Michael fell in to shotgun, slamming the door behind. "Go!"

Alex turned the ignition and pulled away, the tyres screeching on the roads wet surface. From the doorway of Jake's house the demented woman appeared, crawling across the ground with bent elbows.

"Oh my God!" Michael shouted as they passed by, barging the wheelchair from their path. "What was that?"

"I don't know."

From between the buildings intermittent light flashed. About them, above them, the light continued, snapping in silence like a paparazzi flashbulb.

"Get us back to the station. Fast!" A haze of purple and green blotches obscured Michael's vision.

The snow glided past like stars as the car ploughed along Main Street.

"Dispatch? Dispatch! Come in! Over!" The silent electrical storm smothered their vehicle, illuminating the fog from all directions. "What was the light?" Michael asked, feeling nerves quake within his throat.

"I don't know!" Alex snapped. Michael looked at him. Concern had embraced his calm demeanour.

"Dispatch? Come in? Over." The radio whirred and hissed. "Dammit!"

About them a light emerged behind the snow clouds. "I don't believe it!"

"My God," Michael whispered. The cloud warmed with an amber hue. "Again? The sky, again?"

The summer haze engulfed the fog, illuminating the town as it had done so often before. Michael watched as the snowflakes danced against orange clouds. A figure watched them from the sidewalk. "Alex!"

"What?"

"Stop the car!"

They screeched to a halt, the engine purring as they sat upon the tarmac. "What?"

"I swear I just saw…" he opened the door and stepped in to the cold air.

"Michael!"

Michael drew his gun, heading toward the area the figure had been standing.

"Tad? Is that you?" The breeze rattled his clothes, rippling them as it pushed by. "Tad?"

"Michael! Get in the God-damned car!" He turned, seeing Alex step out of the vehicle. Electric snapped and crackled beyond his vision. "Michael!"

Scouring the area one final time, he cussed, running back to the car.

"I swear to God I saw Tad Williams on the sidewalk back there."

Alex dropped the transmission in to gear and pulled away. "I don't know what you saw, but we have to get out of here, and hope the station is how we left it."

They pulled in to the station parking lot. Sheriff Palmer and their colleagues stood outside, watching the storm. The sense of panic his officers exuded encouraged him to order everyone back inside. For some reason he order the building secure. Every window, and every door. Something was wrong, and it frightened him.

## 30

"My friends, the time is now upon us. This dawn, this breaking of a new day, signals what is about to befall the small town of Millers Fall. It is the first step in a long journey, a journey we have wandered for so many years. A journey where the destination is our reward. The destination is life; our life, the way we live. A life in which we may live in peace and free from fear. For it is the will of those we watch, those whom we worked so hard to appease, to wander this plain as and when they wish, and no longer will anyone have the power to stop them."

Mitchum Hoyt stood upon the porch looking out to his sea of followers. Snow lingered within long hair and unkempt beards. It danced about them as they stood watching, appearing as shadows within the snowfall, carrying candles or lamps to guide their eyes.

Surrounded by his bearded generals, Mister McCallum and Altman, Hoyt grasped the handrail and stepped down to the snow-sodden grass surrounding his home.

"We have done what we can. We have played our part, but society must now accept its fate. We will move forward, for we have not sinned. We can live free from fear, and know that whatever happens to society has happened of its own doing, and that we are free from judgement." The surrounding woods came to life. Branches roared within the gusts of a cold breeze. Patchy fog danced about the backwoods clan. A crow cawed in the distance. In fact, as he peered about his home, they roosted on every available surface. Dark messengers engulfed the decayed tractor just beyond his people and nestled upon the beams of his home. Ten, twenty, thirty, maybe even forty, flapped their wings, ruffled feathers or cawed from their perches, arriving as silent and hidden as a ghosts, only drawing attention now they wished to be seen.

"It is a sign," Hoyt whispered, no longer caring to address his people. He looked from one murder to the other as each beady, dark eye peered back. "There will be death this very day. Samael, the ferrier of souls, draws near."

## 31

Michael burst in to the office. "Sheriff! Quick! Something's going down outside!"

Palmer frowned. "What?" The urgency about his officer was enough to draw concern.

"I have no idea, sir. Screaming, explosions, I don't know what!"

Palmer leapt from his chair. Joined by Brooks, they entered the offices and walked in to the corridor. The station entrance was open. Alex stood outside, his gun drawn.

"What? What is it?" Brooks asked as they stepped out in to the cold air.

Alex held a hand out. "Listen," he whispered.

Palmer peered as far as the snow allowed, turning his focus to a different sense. The wind passed in gentle gusts, howling across his ears, but that was all.

"I don't hear anything," Brooks whispered.

Alex turned to him. "That's the problem. There's nothing."

Michael wandered across to his partner. "The street was full of screaming, alarms, and God knows what else a few seconds ago!"

Palmer gazed upon the patrol car sat vacant on the road. "Deputy, take the car. Head out and see what's up."

Diana burst out of the building. "Sheriff! Lines are down. Signals are down. Everything's dead." The lights about the building flickered.

Palmer turned, watching as the station lost power, falling to a stormy gloom without even a whimper. "The hell?"

Brooks descended the steps and opened his patrol car. He'd not long arrived for his shift and appeared ready to tackle whatever was thrown at him. The officers peered down as the engine ticked. One turn, two turns…it roared on the third.

"Where do you want me to go?" he shouted.

"Just up and down. Not far. We have no contact with you, so watch yourself."

Brooks jumped in to the driver's seat and pulled away, closing the door whilst moving.

"I have a real bad feeling about this," Alex said as the rear lights vanished in to the cloud.

"Me too," Diana whispered.

"Keep your heads together," Palmer ordered, "this is what we do."

Vehicle twenty two hummed as Brooks passed out of sight. The atmosphere was one of anxiety. The silence that engulfed The Fall told its own story. Each officer stood, listening as Deputy Brooks drove further in to the snow. The engine diminished with every second that passed. Motionless they waited, curious to what he may find.

Tyres screamed through the fog as Brooks slammed the brakes. "Shit!" Michael shouted, descending the steps.

"Wait!" Palmer snapped. His gut lurched. Something was wrong. "Wait." Palmer glared to Michael, making his point. The officer complied and stopped, standing on the steps. From across the distance the car rumbled. The siren blipped and wailed, hidden beyond the falling snow before powering down to a mysterious silence. Goosebumps spread across Palmer's flesh.

"What's he doing?" Diana asked.

The siren blipped, this time whirring with a different tone. Erratic sounds and prolonged whines emanated within the cloud.

"Siren's don't do that," Alex replied.

Michael clasped hands behind his neck. "You think he's okay?"

The siren ceased. Nervousness fluttered about the station. Palmer didn't answer. Not because he couldn't, but chose not to. The regret at sending Brooks out swirled about him, tapping his thoughts at every opportunity.

The snow illuminated, bursting with light. Burning, white flashes emanated across the distance. Electricity snapped out of sight, pulsating about the officers with the crackle of raw energy.

"Move!"

The patrol car flew through the air, rotating as it smashed to the ground. Palmer dived, crashing to the concrete surface. Smashed glass and shattered metal pierced the silence. The siren blipped. Steam hissed, escaping from unknown components. The horn sounded. An alarm engaged. All hell broke loose.

Palmer shook the fuzz from his brain. The twisted frame of a patrol car rested not ten feet away.

"Anthony! You okay?" Diana recovered from the raining vehicle and rushed across to the driver's side.

Deputy Brooks slumped across the wheel, barley conscious.

"Deputy!" Palmer shouted. Blood streamed from an open wound above his apprentices ear. "Anthony! Can you hear me?"

Brooks turned. "Yes," he whispered.

"Okay. Come on, we gotta get you out of there."

The vehicle's side had been dented and bent. Palmer grabbed the handle, and with brute force prized the door open. It creaked and fell, unable to sustain the damage it received. Brooks fell back in the chair, halting the drone of the horn. The seat belt had been engaged. *'Lucky for you,'* Palmer thought. *'Remember, kids. Seatbelts save lives.'* No other wound appeared on the Deputy, except for lacerations to his head.

"You hurt anywhere?"

Brooks turned to him with puppy-dog eyes. "My legs gone."

Palmer looked around. Alex and Michael lurched to their feet. "Guys! Get here. Give me a hand." He turned back to his Deputy. "We'll get you out."

They removed Brooks from the wreck, supporting him either side. He winced as they stood. "My leg. It's done."

"Sheriff," came Diana's voice. She alerted his attention to the plethora of lamplight twinkling within the snow. At the front, Mitchum Hoyt appeared.

"Is this you're doing?" Palmer snapped.

Hoyt chuckled in his usual, infamous way. "Do I look like I can hurl a vehicle?" All about him the lamps glittered. "No, sir, it was not me. But do I know who did it? The answer is most certainly yes."

"Who, then?"

Hoyt opened his arms. "Those beings to which your town now belongs."

"You're every bit as crazy as everyone believes."

"Ha. No, sir, I am not. They engulf your town, along every street, inside every home. All except this building. Your workplace. Your sanctuary." Palmer looked back at the station. "Sheriff, you must make a decision. It is a very important decision, too, and one that regards our two trigger happy friends currently residing in your cells."

"I don't do deals," Palmer retorted. Brooks cried out.

"Oh, but you will," Hoyt growled. No longer was he the jester. "If you want to live." As if sensing his own malevolence, he grunted then chuckled. "But, as I said, the decision is yours."

Palmer turned his back. "Go to Hell."

A raucous, amusement filled laugh bellowed from the sidewalk. "I have no need to, Sheriff. Hell has come here." Palmer turned back. Hoyt stared with a bitten lip and flared nostrils. "I want both of them, the murderer and his culprit. We will exact our own justice for Miss Olivia."

"You'll kill them."

"What we do is no concern of yours!" Hoyt extended an arm. His index finger singled out the Sheriff. "I will give you time. When I return, I will take them with me. You and your friends will be spared."

Palmer stood defiant. "And if I refuse?"

Hoyt grinned. "Then you will die. You must consider which is more important. Your lives, or your prisoners. In the meantime, they'll send an old friend, or *friends*, to help you decide."

The cult leader tipped his fedora and stepped back in to the lamplight. Each lantern faded, twinkling like starlight, until nothing but snowflakes existed where the lights once floated.

***

"Shit! Shit!" Brooks gasped as he settled down. Alex and Michael helped him to the floor. His broken leg flopped to the side.

"Diana, stay with him." Palmer gestured for the partners to join him. "Listen, arm yourselves, stay here. I want you looking out for anything suspicious out there. Get Anthony some pain killers. There's some usually found in or around the first aid box. We can't evac or get medical assistance in while the weather's this bad."

"Fantastic," Michael whispered.

Palmer sighed. "Let's just try and make it comfortable for him. Well, as best as we can. You both do that, I'm heading downstairs. I think I need to talk with our suspects."

***

"Sheriff, what in the blue hell is going on up there?" Terry sat upon the wooden bench installed to the holding cell. Through the bars he peered, sat beside his cohort, Buck.

"Are you boys coming to term with what you did?"

"For God's sake, Sheriff, she got in the damn way!"

"You two have no idea of the problems you've caused! We are in the middle of the worst storm to ever hit The Fall. I have no communication with the outside world. I have a seriously injured officer, and three others holding the fort. You know what else I have?

How about Mitchum Hoyt and his cult demanding I release you to their custody so they can exact their own form of judgement on you."

"Screw them," Buck retorted. "We'll take them all down, do the town a favour."

"That's what you don't understand!" Palmer shouted. "There's no way I can keep the law against a clan of thirty plus people. I mean, damn. If I don't hand you over, they're gonna march in here and take you anyway."

Terry smiled. "I don't believe it, Sheriff. You really are a coward." Buck roared from his side. "I mean, everyone speaks of you hiding behind that badge of yours, but it's actually true. First sign of trouble and you soil yourself."

Palmer seethed at the hunters. Maybe these assholes would be better off in the hands of the backwoods cult. "Terry, neither you nor Buck are what I'm concerned with at this moment in time." He walked past as they laughed, and passed the cell where Finn met his fate. Remnants of his blood still existed in a pale haze, where cleaning products and chemicals had been beaten. He moved to the holding cell that housed a single occupant. Cane peered through the white bars.

"Mister Cane. We need to talk."

Palmer sat down at the table, yet again in the damned interrogation room. Agent Cane sat opposite, his hands clasped upon the surface.

"You know what's going on, don't you?"

Cane nodded. "Yep. Pretty much."

"You want to fill me in?"

"Ah, I don't think you'd believe me."

Palmer placed his elbows on the table. "Mister Cane, as I said to you earlier, this week I've seen sunsets at midnight, snowstorms instead of sunshine and people tortured beyond recognition, but still they were able to live. Add to that a police officer spewing blood and rolling up the walls like some damned Reagan McNeill, and now an entire town's population that seems to have just vanished, and I may just believe you, even if you told me that Slender Man was behind it all."

Cane smiled. "Slender Man is an internet creation. It's amazing how many people think he's actually real."

"Mister Cane, I need you to talk to me, and let me know what's happening here." Palmer kept his cool, almost polite in his approach, knowing Cane was now the only person who could shed some light on what was happening.

The look on Cane's face expressed some kind of concern. How sincere it was could be debated.

"Alright," the agent replied, mirroring Palmer's coolness, "Aliens. That's what it is. Well, that's what we call them, anyway."

They sat in an uncomfortable silence. Cane appeared to be awaiting a response. Maybe telling his story had been met with distain in the past? Palmer had sure-as-hell dismissed it.

"Not the Russians, then? Or the Koreans?" Palmer almost wished it was.

"No, Extra Terrestrial life from another planet."

There seemed a stern expression on Cane's face, now. No twitching, no flapping. He appeared tired, but with no sign to mislead. Palmer nodded. "Go on."

"This world is not the only world populated by intelligent beings. There are others, too. They're far, far away."

"In a galaxy, I'm guessing?"

Cane smiled. "But not a long time ago. These worlds are thriving as we speak." Palmer shifted on the chair. "Now, because we are on different planets, we rarely come in to contact. Think of a building that has a ground floor, a first floor and a second floor. Now imagine that those floors are locked, and no-one can enter or leave. We walk around on the ground floor." Cane placed his fingers on the table and walked them across the surface. "We might hear the bumps and bangs coming from above us, or see some kind of activity that indicate there's people up there, in our case the sky, but we don't ever see anything to suggest otherwise. When we do, it's what everyone calls a UFO. And sometimes, if an opportunity arises, a person from that floor above can find a way down to our level."

Palmer sat back. "Explain to me your concept of floors."

"Ground level is Earth. It's life. It's us, just seeing out our lives however we choose to do so. Level one is everything above us; the sky, space, all that area," Cane flapped his hand, "and level two is their own planet. Now, it's no secret that aliens are highly advanced creatures, more so than anyone from the human race. You don't need me to tell you that, the Discovery Channel has probably done it already. Imagine what happens when a creature of significant intelligence, and I mean an even higher functioning individual or individuals from their species, decides to study the lower life forms within the universe."

"Is that what you're telling me? That we're being studied by aliens?"

Cane sighed. "There's truth behind the stories, Sheriff. That's why our government laughs off cases of abduction and sightings of lights in the sky. I mean, who do you think it is that makes those shows? The more fantastical the account, the more the average person doesn't believe. It's genius, I'll give them that."

"So, people get abducted for experiments?" Palmer's mind recalled Finn and his recollection of lights and screaming. An image of Tina, her gut stapled together whilst organs pushed to escape, filled his mind. Cane's theory was farfetched, but it now made sense.

"Yep, Sheriff, but this time there's something different about your case here in Millers Fall. We've had transporters fall before, that's nothing new, but I was dispatched because they're lingering. They've got a real interest in this place."

"Why has everyone vanished? I mean, surely a space ship can't hold the population of an entire town?"

"Is that what's happened?"

"The handful of staff I have on duty have not gained contact from anyone. No visual, verbal or otherwise. The town appears dead. Michael and Alex reported a woman creeping up from a puddle of blood-"

"Shit!" Cane leapt from the table. "When? Where?" His hands found Palmer's shoulders.

"About an hour ago."

"Crap, Sheriff! This is a real situation you find yourself in. This is dangerous."

"What? What is she?"

"A humanoid form. A terrible creature." Cane exhaled and looked to gain some composure. "Imagine your mind flowing through the air without a body. That's what this creature is, only it will find an element then take a form. In this case it found a puddle of blood." Cane placed a hand on his forehead. He wandered the room for a moment, as though it were he interrogating the Sheriff. He pushed his hands together, as though in prayer, and waved them back and forth. "Okay. If it's here, it suggests she may be looking for something. That would be why it hasn't moved on."

"What?" Palmer enquired.

"It has to be something worthwhile. But, there's also going to be someone to help. All beings need eyes and ears on the ground floor. A corrupted mind, you know? Someone who has been influenced?"

Palmer knew in an instant.

"Mitchum Hoyt."

"Sheriff, your comet was a transporter. It was a capsule containing the creature."

"Cane, I'm not bothered with how it got here. What I need to know is how to deal with it."

Cane sighed. His hands rested atop his hips. "There's nothing you can do. She'll wipe out this area looking for what she wants."

"But if we find it? If we give it to her?"

175

Cane raised his brows. "Maybe. But finding it is gonna prove difficult, and there's no knowing if she'll leave us in peace afterward."

Palmer pushed himself from the table. A thought crossed his mind. Could he do it? Could he actually go through with it?

"I think I know what she's after."

Cane looked at him. "Really?"

"Yes, but I'm not sure I can do it."

"Sheriff, I don't think you understand the situation. At this moment, all of us are going to die. Do you understand? That means me, you, your staff, everyone left. If there's a chance you can stop that, I'd advise you to consider your position."

Palmer walked across to the door, grasping the cold handle. "Even if it means sending two men to their deaths?"

## 32

Tad wandered the orange fog. The cold snapped at his arms and hands, but otherwise found himself comfortable within the orange snow. He'd heard screams, crashes, full blown chaos and taken to hide behind a dumpster, but now a sense of calm had gripped The Fall, so much so that his confidence had returned.

He knew that somewhere around here the police station lurked, but wanted to avoid it, in case Mom had reported him missing. Something had to be going on, as Officer Michael York had jumped from his vehicle and called out. Tad had done a great job avoiding anyone. Even Denny's Store had been empty. A couple of bucks had hidden themselves deep inside his pockets, and upon finding them he'd decided to head there and grab some candy. When an empty shop provides you with a full cash register and no guards, an opportunist will take advantage. Not only did his rucksack burst to capacity, but his pockets did, too. He had plenty of cash to buy a bus ticket out of here and hire a motel somewhere for a few nights. His lips curled in to a smile. Maybe it was a sign? Maybe this was his destiny?

Tad returned to consciousness. He'd been wandering on autopilot, and found himself past the station and heading out of The Fall. It was so quiet. So still....

A gurgle caught his attention. Someone choked. Somewhere, hidden behind the fog and snowflakes, someone needed help. The choke turned to a cough, as if a fur-ball regurgitated from a throat, but not that of an animal. It sounded human.

Tad studied the direction from which it emanated. Something was happening. The thin layer of snow now resting across The Fall creaked as feet trudged through its crispness. A rasp drew inward. A breath. Behind him....

He smashed in to the ground, legs trailing in the air. The snow felt cold and uncomfortable as he writhed within the element, dazed and disorientated. A bony, clawed hand reached out, grasping at his chest before twisting the material of his hoodie. He rose from the ground, peering in to blank, dark eyes. Without even knowing, he fumbled inside his jeans for the marble. The face of a witch glared back at him. Dark, shady sockets and wrinkled, pale skin filled his vision. A nose, long and pointed reached down to an open mouth full of shards. The creature crackled, as though mucus nestled inside its throat. Tad fought with his pocket as a clawed finger tickled his now exposed abdomen. The pressure increased....

Its attention snapped to the side, to the hand that grasped the sphere, then looked back to him. An expression of shock engulfed its grotesque features. Tad slumped to the floor. His clothes became matted in blood, although himself, he felt no injury. The gangling, sexless, horrendous woman peered down. She knelt at his side, her palms open. Tad panted, but now the fear he'd felt had vanished, and as the creature tended him, became content. A long hand took hold of his jaw with the most delicate of touches. She'd noticed something. With a gentle movement Tad rolled his head to the side, allowing the creature to investigate the bruises that Sam had inflicted. She returned his gaze to hers, and whilst holding his chin took her other palm and stroked his hair. Snowflakes nestled in her long, matted strands as they peered to one another. Her body quivered. She snarled. The elongated hands released him as she stood, and became enraged. He didn't know how he knew, he just did. He felt her anger.

The creature shook and trembled until she exploded, throwing her head back in the most horrendous scream he'd ever heard. Tad closed his eyes and covered his ears. Even subdued, the wail filled his mind. It screeched through the fog and snowfall, as though a Banshee foretold the death of someone close.

She stopped. Tad opened his eyes. Blood plastered the snow about him. The cold air attacked in gusts, but the creature had gone.

"Shit!" It's coming!" Cane screeched as they joined the others.

"What is?" Alex asked.

Palmer looked down to him, crouched beside Brooks. "No time to explain." He peered about the reception. "Are we secure?"

"Yes," Diana began, un-holstering her pistol. "Everywhere is locked down. No one can get in from anywhere but through here."

The station stood solid. All windows at the rear had bars in place on the lower levels, and a huge, steel door that lead out of the back entrance to the parking lot.

"This is the only area Hoyt can target, unless of course he has explosives." Palmer regretted even having the thought.

"It's tough if he has. We can only prepare for so much." Michael added. He had a point.

Palmer nodded. "Screw it. We do what we can." He turned to the newly released comrade. "This is Agent Cane. He's here to help, and has experience with everything that's going on. Don't ask too many questions now, but follow his lead. That's an order."

The officers looked to him. They didn't appear judgemental, just happy to have a leader.

"I have one question," Michael asked as he peered out in to the snow. "Why did the sky turn orange?"

Cane turned to Palmer, appearing to gain permission. Palmer nodded.

"Lights."

"Lights?" he asked. "From what?"

"A ship."

A stunned silence engulfed the room. Brooks yelped out, his face contorting in pain.

Alex giggled. "A space ship? Are you for real?"

"We don't have time for this," Palmer began, moving to the window. He stood beside Michael and checked the surroundings. "We're gonna have a clan of pissed off hillbillies return any minute, prepared to take two prisoners. They're gonna use force. We have that creature out there looking for those..." Palmer stopped. A thought had surged through his mind. "Cane, why are they both looking for the same two people?"

"You mean you haven't figured it out yet?"

Palmer's mind ticked. It placed together, as simple as a kid's jigsaw puzzle. "She was one," he replied. "She was one, and they killed her."

"I think so. I believe you have one or two that have infiltrated your community. Look at it. Quiet town in the middle of nowhere. Who'd know?"

"Damn." Palmer caught Diana looking to him, and threw her a bunch of keys. "Go get them. Hand them their weapons and bring them here."

"Are you sure about that?" Alex asked.

"We need all the help we can get. This is going to be a standoff, you realise?" He turned to Diana. "Go!"

"But...."

"No buts, Alex." Palmer replied in an unusual, calm tone. "Go to the armoury and bring everything you can hold. Take Agent Cane with you. Michael and I will stand guard until then."

With no objection, Alex disappeared through a door with the Agent.

"Shit!" Michael exclaimed, moving back from the window. "We go movement."

Palmer moved to the pane. Shadows emerged from the falling snow. One, two, three....

He studied them as they emerged and stood at the base of the steps.

"Benny?" Michael asked. Palmer looked to him. "That's Benny. And, and Oscar." The officer became erratic. "Max?"

"What?" Palmer sighed. The pale, abysmal figures that stood before the station now appeared a husk of their former selves. They stood like zombies, almost lifeless as snowflakes caught their clothes and passed in a flurry about them. Two more figures emerged.

"No way," Michael whispered. "It's them."

Palmer uttered no response as the shadows loomed in to view. "Brent? Jason?"

The missing teens loomed into view, their bodies too, a shell of what they once were. Each figure stood meaningless within the storm.

"It's the missing." Michael dashed across to the door.

"No!" Palmer screamed.

"But Sheriff-"

"No. It's a trap. They're bait."

Michael stood against the door. "But they're alive."

Palmer shook his head. "No, not any more. Look at them." Michael joined him at the window. Both peered out at their audience. "There's nothing living about them. See? They'll be like Finn. Dead."

Palmer noticed a flash of light dance about the missing. They did not flinch. Lightning flashed and wrapped about them, snapping and thrashing like an enraged serpent, yet still they did not flinch. The lightning burned white, its aura growing in strength until his eyes needed shielding. White shafts streamed in through the windows. Michael stumbled. A soft explosion, one after the other, popped within the whiteout. A flutter of thuds rained against the building.

Palmer turned, shielding his eyes. The foundations rattled. The ground quaked. He slumped to the ground. Michael groaned. He swayed as the earthquake took hold, jarring the building. Plaster rained from the ceiling. The pungent aroma of dust engulfed the air. Glass smashed. The light faded.

"Sheriff!" came Diana's voice through the carnage.

He managed to stand. The station came to a standstill. Fallen debris littered the ground. Lights from the ceiling, chairs and plaster now littered the reception.

"Oh God!" Buck cried, pointing to the windows. Palmer turned. Crimson blobs and claret streaks adorned the panes. His heart sank. Brooks cried out.

"See him," Palmer said to Diana, gesturing toward his Deputy. Buck and Terry were loaded. Palmer withdrew his handgun. "You boys ready?" Terry appeared wild and frightened, his eyes wide and mouth agape, yet still he nodded. "Michael, open the door. I want to see what happened out there."

"What?"

"Just open the God-damned door! Buck and Terry are going to cover. You got it?" This time both hunters nodded. Palmer turned to the entrance. "Now!"

# 33

"I will fear no evil as I walk this life that has been bestowed upon me. I repel the haters, the accusers, the ones who condemned me from the basic right to life, and thus began a fresh, looking to the stars for guidance. And, of course, they provided. We have been provided for, my brethren. We have been nurtured for decades, and now we stand, inches from our place in existence, not just the world. Shangri-La? Heaven? Hedonism? What awaits us? What will we discover? Unless our minds are open we will not see what has been chosen, and to do so, we must bring the two sinners with us on our journey. Our worlds have been united and now we must deliver, or we will miss the glory of above. We move. We take what is required and let nothing stand in our way, be it a storm, an element or a man. We move *now*, take those two men and let nothing stop us. Then, and only then, will our perseverance be rewarded." Mitchum Hoyt turned from his people and looked in to the snowfall. The lamp he carried illuminated the path. "Come. Now is the time."

***

Palmer stood outside his station. Sorrow passed through every inch of his being as he peered out in to the madness. The entire sidewalk, now awash with blood, housed flesh and organs where the missing once stood. A severed hand here, a missing tooth there. An eyeball, a dark mass, liver or lung, who knew? From the streetlight tattered flesh flapped in the breeze carrying the snowfall. A flake nestled on his cheek, alerting his senses and drawing him back. Palmer brushed the residue away with a finger, watching as the pure, white elements fluttered to the ground, covering the crimson carnage in a thin veil of purity.

"Good Lord above," Palmer sighed, still unable to comprehend the debauchery surrounding him.

"Not him," a voice replied in the distance. He looked up. A plethora of lamps approached through the snowfall. "Although he may have forsaken you." Silhouettes loomed in grey mass beyond the elements, each taking human form. Hoyt and his followers wandered between the snowflakes. Many carried weapons; guns, machetes, and their lamps.

Hoyt held out an arm, stopping those that followed, somewhere in the middle of the road that used to exist before the storm came.

"Sheriff. I think you know why we are here. I see you have them ready." Palmer turned to the station doors where Buck and Terry stood, their rifles aiming toward the sea of judges. "Now, if you'd be as kind as to hand them over, we will attempt to rectify this most horrible situation that has cascaded over your beloved town."

The rage of conflict battled inside. Palmer wanted to hand the hunters across so bad, but his morals engaged in an attempt to protect justice. He looked from the hunters, who glared back, to the madman and his followers, all peering to him within the soft light of their lanterns.

"Come now, Sheriff. Surly it cannot be such a difficult decision?"

"What the hell are you doing, Sheriff? Tell them to get lost," Terry shouted. The fear in his voice stood out as bright and clear as the lamps behind the snow.

"Sheriff?" Hoyt asked in a malevolent tone. "Tick-tock."

Palmer closed his eyes. He felt his colleagues' eyes watching from the station. The power of his heart rattled inside, bursting with energy. The pounding noise it made submerged his ears.

"Sheriff?" Terry asked.

Palmer looked to him.

Buck sighed. "Screw this!"

"No!" A gunshot rattled in to the clan. Terry followed suit. About them the air filled with gunfire. "Get in!" Palmer screamed, pushing the hunters through the door. Gunfire emanated from the lamp-bearers. Mortar exploded in to dust as bullets rained upon them. Palmer stumbled in to the station. Michael slammed the door and barred it.

"What the hell were you thinking?" Alex shouted, taking aim with a shotgun through a window. The thud of bullets surrounded the officers as they sheltered inside.

"Get to a window!" Palmer bellowed, pushing Buck to the front of the building. He and Terry dashed across to the nearest, beside Deputy Brooks. Palmer rushed across to him, placing his pistol in to the Deputy's palm. "Anyone comes through that door, kill them," he ordered. Brooks nodded.

"They're moving in!" Michael shouted, protecting the same window as Alex.

"Keep them back!" Cane ordered.

"I bagged me one!" Terry shouted. "Yeehaw!"

Palmer tipped the sofa on to the floor, back down against the floor. "Diana, cover here." She ran across within the hail of bullets and took cover. "Protect Brooks," he said, peering around the edge. She nodded.

Light penetrated the doors with each bullet that passed through. "They're taking cover behind the steps!" Alex shouted, releasing two rounds outside.

Palmer found the stash of ammunition and weapons he had collected with Agent Cane, and threw a box of shells across. Michael reloaded.

"What are you firing?" he shouted to Buck.

Buck released fire outside before taking cover. "Ruger American."

"Him?" Palmer pointed to Terry, who fired from the window. "Sako Finnlight."

Palmer brushed through the ammunition. "Damn it. I've got nothing for them."

"Did you leave it in the truck?"

Palmer ignored the question. Instead, he grasped one of the Remington 870's. "Here," he shouted, tossing it through the air.

Buck caught it with one hand. "What the hell is this shit?"

"I ain't using no shotgun!" Terry whined.

"Fine. The place needed redecorating anyway."

Buck shook his head. He reached out for the ammunition. Palmer threw it across.

"Shit! We got a ram!" Alex screamed.

"Bring him down!" Cane bellowed. Sprinting, heavy footfalls battered the steps outside. "Bring him down!"

The doors exploded as a body surged through, knocking one clear from its hinges. Palmer slammed against a wall, his gut aching from the strike. Within a daze, the double image of the monster hidden by a burlap sack appeared.

"Get him!" a voice screeched. The weapons turned on the infiltrator, but not before he took hold of Terry. The hunter squealed, taken and thrown outside in to the snow.

"Tez!" Buck screamed.

Bullets rippled the giants body as he stood, absorbing the punishment. Blood exploded from his flesh. Buck took hold of the shotgun and point blank pulled the trigger. The sack exploded, searing bone and matter throughout the room. Pink flesh splattered against the walls. The body smashed down with a thud. A cry warbled from outside.

"They've got him!" Michael shouted.

"Take them down," Palmer replied, wincing as he stood.

"I've lost visual."

The gunfire ceased. In a moment of calm they took cover. Buck was alive, as were Michael and Alex. Cane was fine too. Diana appeared sturdy. Brooks....

Palmer moved across to his Deputy. He sat, back to the wall, head to the side. The handgun inside his palm lay un-grasped. His chest bled.

Palmer sighed, looking away. After a moment he turned back, closing the Deputy's eyes. "Rest easy."

The southern accent drifted from outside. "Sheriff!"

Anger surged within his veins. Palmer squeezed the Glock. Everyone inside the station looked to him. He stood, turned and made for the exit.

"Wait! You can't just go out there!" Cane pleaded, attempting to block his way.

"Out of the way!" he snapped, pushing the Agent with force.


Bodies littered the steps and sidewalk. Blood seeped in to the snow. Lanterns lay on their sides, some holding light, some diminished. Hoyt appeared in the road, again followed by his clan. There must be ten, fifteen bodies out here, but still the police remained outnumbered.

"Sheriff, we have one. Hand across the other and we will leave you." Hoyt appeared troubled, as though something played on his conscience.

"Why?" Palmer asked, flapping his gun to the chaos that had adorned his doorstep. "Can't you see what we've done? What *you've* done?" Hoyt looked upon the battlefield.

"Sheriff, you have no idea what is happening right now."

Palmer gave a smile. "Enlighten me."

"Your fate is twinned with ours, whether you like it or not."

"What is it with you, and speaking in damned riddles?" he asked, scrunching his face in confusion. "Can you speak English, or something that I can understand?"

"Your fate is the same as ours, if you co-operate. You see, we're no longer in Millers Fall."

Palmer coughed, which turned to a laugh. "Really? So that station up there is not here? The bodies on the floor aren't on the sidewalk?"

"This is a preparation, Sheriff. It started with your hunter friends, the one who murdered our Miss Olivia. Everyone not involved with that atrocity still exist, on a different plain. In fact, it is not the townsfolk who vanished, but instead the people involved." Hoyt became judgemental. "It was you, Sheriff. It was you, all along, with your justice and power to protect the innocents. But that is the problem! Those men are not innocents!" he screamed.

This much Palmer could understand. "Yes. Yeah, I know."

"Then you'll understand that everyone who played a part in her murder has been isolated. That means all of us." Hoyt turned to his followers. His finger then found the Sheriff. "And all of you." A cackle bellowed from his mouth, jarring the beard as he rolled. "You're all too far gone, now. You will either die or enter paradise, with me. The choice is yours. Be one of us," Hoyt said, opening a palm. "Join us and live in Hedonism. For we are many..."

A wail of grief pierced through the snowfall. Its sharp tone and power echoed along the street and across the bodies. Every nook, every corner became penetrated by its ferocity. Hoyt's eyes narrowed. "Alas, it is too late." Palmer looked to the snow, where the scream emerged. "Go, Sheriff. Give yourself one last hurrah. Here comes Death, and it's coming for you."

The scream echoed again, bellowing throughout the battlefield. Palmer turned and headed back to the station.

"What's going on?" Cane asked.

"I don't know, just ready your weapons."

"We can't win this," Alex sighed, peering out at the clan, "they're numbers are too great."

"It's not them I'm worried about."

Alex frowned. "Then what?"

"Whatever it is out there making that noise. Hoyt thinks it's the angel of death."

## 34

Hoyt stood within the snowfall, his clothing saturated from the element. The cold did not trouble him, he was too preoccupied. The scream ceased, leaving him to lead his people.

"Soon, my friends. Soon." He looked about their faces. Some afraid, some at ease, and some of which he couldn't read. Terry had been taken hostage at the rear. His struggles against two bearded men had drawn attention. A sense of unease passed over the leader.

"What are you going to do with me?" Terry snapped, all the while being restrained.

"Not me," Hoyt replied. "Them." He scoured the sky, as though his eye penetrated the density of the clouds. "Release him." His attention turned to the prisoner. "Release him, please." The men did as requested and relaxed their hold, allowing Terry to struggle free.

"You bastards," he began, walking around the clan. "You wait until I get my gun." Without even a scream he vanished in to the fog. No noise, no indication, no nothing. Mid-walk he disappeared. People in the area looked about. Murmurings began.

"Do not worry," Hoyt said, drawing their attention back. "We are safe." Some engaged their weapons. They parted, taking a defensive stance against the hidden threat. "They are not here for us."

A yelp burst through the snow. Legs vanished in to the fog as someone jarred from their standing point. Screams sailed from the cloud, telling a story of pain and suffering. The remaining backed away.

"What are you doing?" Hoyt snapped. "We are protected!"

Mister McAllum wandered to the back, peering in to the fog. His eye followed the barrel of a shotgun as he scoured the area.

"Mister McAllum, what do you see?" Hoyt asked from a distance. McAllum turned, grasping the barrel of his weapon. From the fog loomed a hand, larger than any Hoyt had seen before. Pale skin led to long, dark claws. Its fingers opened above McAllum's head.

"Nothing."

The hand smashed on to McAllum, taking his head within its palm. With one swift movement it withdrew, carrying Hoyt's general in to the fog. Gunfire exploded around them. His people screamed. They dispersed, running in a wild and eccentric frenzy. Electricity pulsed within the orange fog. Lightning snapped and thrashed within the breeze. Bodies exploded, as if grenades had been swallowed after their pins pulled. Blood rained down upon the ground as one after the other they blew, each in the most brutal way. Hoyt stood, his heart pounding, as one after the other the family he created fell to the ground in a rain of blood and bone.

"It can't be…." he muttered, frozen to the spot as fear took a hold. Around him the fog fell quiet. Snow attacked him from each side, the cold now stabbing at his body with an iced blade. The silence engulfed him, like the fog, and left him alone. As Hoyt stood, peering in to the elements with fear, the sense of isolation became stronger than he had ever experienced.

Scraping emerged from the direction he looked. Hoyt, his back to the station, backed away. The noise grew louder, until the ambling shadow of a silhouette appeared within the fog. It towered in to the air, some seven feet tall. Gangly arms and disjointed legs emerged as the snow fluttered down across the bloodshed. Hoyt forgot the bodies that littered about him. He forgot the people he loved. The only thing that now existed, the ambiguous shadow that ambled toward him. Adrenaline surged through his body. Sweat trickled from his temple, even within the winter's storm.

The silhouette loomed from the clouds, revealing the creature from his darkest nightmares. Its long, wild hair matted against a pale skin. A wrinkled face bore a long, thin nose that curled downward. Sunken, dark eye sockets led to black, lifeless eyes. The scraping noise it made came from the leg that dragged within the snow. The creature stopped, noticing Hoyt as he peered back. He trembled, legs quaking as he stood rooted to the spot.

Its head cocked to the side. The dead eyes scoured him.

"He's in there," Hoyt whimpered, raising a judgemental finger to the station. "The one you want. He's in there."

The creatures gaze shifted to the police station. It looked back and forth, from man to building, before engaging its legs and moving once more.

It approached him. Hoyt could do nothing but stare. The grotesque life-form ambled past, ignoring him as though he did not exist, appearing as a titan beneath the snowfall.

The distorted creature reached the base of the steps. Hoyt drew in, his breaths reduced to rapid rasps. Tingling sensations passed throughout his chest. The creature gurgled, and looked back. Hoyt found the eyes staring over him once more.

She turned.

Hoyt turned, now able to move. He sprinted as fast as the bulbous torso would allow, running blind in to the fog. The creature's footfalls crunched through the snow behind before reaching out. A clawed hand slammed down and smashed him in to the blanket. Plumes of white cloud expelled in to the air. She grasped his head, lifting him clear of the ground. Hoyt screamed, his legs swaying as he grasped at the claw. She took hold of his thigh and pulled in opposite directions.

His vertebrae snapped. Pain seared the back of his head. He wailed. Skin stretched. Ligaments snapped. The screams tone shifted higher and higher, from a man, to a girl, to an infant...

The creature threw his body across the bloodshed, keeping a hold of his decapitated head. It still wore the fedora, kept in place by the power of her grip. Hoyt's mouth opened and closed in minute movements, bobbing like a fish out of water. The expression on his face, wild and terrified, suggested he may still be conscious.

## 35

"What the hell are we going to do?" Alex shouted.

"Shoot it!" Palmer screamed.

The reception room exploded with the sound of shell and bullets exploding from its confines.

Alex, Michael, Buck, Diana, and Cane joined in unleashing round after round, attempting to thwart the creature that approached.

Her body jarred, jolting with each round that connected. Ripples of blood exploded from her body, knocking the creature off course as she waded through the snow.

Diana frowned. "It should be dead!"

"Just keep going!" Cane replied.

The hail of bullets blew flesh from her frame, but still the creature continued. She moved closer, reaching the steps with Hoyt's head still clutched inside her claw. A well placed bullet blew an eye socket away. The creature slumped, rocking to her knees.

"We got it!" Buck screeched.

The gunfire came to a halt. Agent Cane moved to the entrance, peering down upon the creature as it knelt within the snow. Palmer joined him. A sense of unease befell the station. A rare moment of peace emerged that felt somehow strange, like it should not exist. Palmer raised the shotgun toward the creature.

"Is it dead?"

Cane's head shook. "I don't think so."

The creature jerked. Her body contorted and snapped. It growled, low and malevolent as it rose once more.

"We have to get out of here," Cane said advised. "No amount of bullets will stop...."

She screamed, throwing her head toward the sky. The screech pierced Palmer's mind. He dropped the weapon to cover his ears. The wail echoed across The Fall, attacking them and growing stronger.

Palmer fell to his knees, his mind ready to explode. He grimaced, looking to the sky. The snowfall dashed about him within a breeze that rattled down from the heavens. Within the orange shade that engulfed the fog a cluster of oval lights appeared. Beneath them the ground trembled. Once more an earthquake took hold, rattling the building to its foundations. The lights descended, obscured by debris that blasted by in the gusts. The creature shrilled. A mechanical noise appeared; the whirring of machines, the slide of metal. From the skies above a brilliant, white aura exploded to the ground, cascading everything with a tsunami of blinding light.

Palmer turned. "Run!"

He sprinted in to the station. Gunfire exploded around him. The ground swayed like a ship on a turbulent sea, but still he ran, bursting through the reception doors and in to the station. Light filtered through the blinds. Items rattled and fell from their places. Unable to see, he fell to the ground, crawling across the floor before finding shelter beneath a desk. Above him the table thudded with objects as they fell from their places. Unable to do anything more, he placed his hands about his head and curled in to a fetal position. Screams bellowed from outside. He knew from their tone. Cane first, Alex, Michael, Diana, Buck. What was happening? His eyelids screwed together. Tears trickled on his cheeks.

Footfalls approached over the strange, electric pulse that reverberated throughout the building. They drew closer. The desk launched through the air, leaving Palmer peering up to the distorted creature. She roared, swiping down to grab him. He rolled, crunching glass and paper beneath his body before stumbling to his feet and lurching back outside. His only chance now was to sprint for it. He dashed through the reception, hurdled Brooks' body and out in to the snow. Through the snowfall, through the fog, the sky littered with circular and oval shaped lights. Lightning thrashed in every direction about him. Shafts of light seared down in to the snow. Obscured by the flakes, they contained people. Diana in one, Alex another, the last of his force suspended in mid-air within an aura shining from the heavens. A beam struck his body, freezing him in position. He struggled, he screamed, but nothing happened. The sensation of movement began, and beneath his feet the world fell away.

He watched the rest of his group ascending towards the lights. Michael, Buck, Cane and now him.

His last conscious thought was that of sending Jeanette home.

## 36

"Anything?"

"No, sir. Nothing."

"Alright. Keep searching."

Agents Davis and Welsh stood within the station, in the reception room that had literally been destroyed. "What the hell happened here?" Davis asked, looking to the bullet holes that shattered the wall work. The whole place had been annihilated.

"It looks like a bomb exploded," Welsh replied, and he was right. Debris on the ground, exposed pipes and metal, this was like the epicentre of an earthquake.

"Any ideas?" Mayor Shipham asked, wading toward the Agent's as they stood inside the chaos.

Davis looked to the shattered car resting on the steps outside. "No. I got nothing to tell you."

"Surly you would have found something? You know, a body, blood, something like that?"

"We have nothing to report," Agent Welsh replied. "There's nothing within this building and nothing within its radius. It's going to take some good old fashioned detective work to figure out what happened here."

"I just don't get it," Shipham began, placing his hands atop his hip. "It's not like Mason to just up and run. He was so proud of this town and what he achieved here."

"Sir." Davis turned. A forensic officer, clad head to toe in white plastic, approached. The Agent fumbled in a pocket to find some vinyl gloves he'd been issued. "I thought you may want to look at this?"

Davis took the small piece of plastic between his fingers. A photograph of Emmett Cane peered back, confirming his role within the Federal Division of Unidentified Intelligence.

"Shit," he sighed, passing it to Welsh.
"Well, this explains a few things."

## Two Years Later

The Manhattan rain fell as thick and fast as the traffic. Car horns peeped in the distance. Somewhere a siren wailed, but the emergency service it belonged to couldn't be identified.

Tad wandered through the rain, on a street with inadequate lighting. He looked down, attempting to avoid the puddles that adorned the sidewalk.

"Hey. Hey, you."

Tad turned as a trio of men approached.

"Yeah?"

"You got a buck to spare, buddy?"

Tad reached in to his pocket and withdrew a Star Wars wallet. He opened it and thumbed through the wad of notes that resided there.

"Geez," one guy whistled, "you're taking a chance flashing that amount of cash to three guys you don't know."

Tad grinned. "It's okay. I'm not afraid of you."

One of them laughed. "Would you look at this guy," he began, before flicking the blade open on a pocket knife. He took Tad by the throat before waving the tip around his face. "I would be, if I were you."

Tad laughed. "Seriously? Three guys with little knives are supposed to frighten me?" The remaining men revealed their blades.

"Seems like you can afford more than a buck," one stated. "How about we take that wallet off your hands? I've always been a Trekkie myself, but I can live with Star Wars this once."

"Gents, please. You don't want to place me in any danger."

"Or what? You gonna use the force?"

Light exploded from Tad's palm, launching the trio through a chain-link fence and on to a basketball court. Tad looked down to the ring he'd had custom made. The sphere swirled within its grasp.

Tad strolled on to the court. "I want to tell you a bit about myself, so that you can understand my point of view." The guys squirmed upon the saturated ground. The rain rattled his hood. "I am an orphan, and up until a few years ago was raised by a foster family."

"I'm gonna kill you!" one guy snapped, pushing himself upright.

"No you're not. And I'll tell you why. My natural parents, I never knew. However, I did find someone willing to give me the relationship with my kin that I never had."

The thieves brandished their knives. "Too bad they'll never see you again." They charged. Tad stood defiant. Light erupted across the playing surface. An awful, paralysing wail screeched between the buildings. The light subsided, revealing the three men stood motionless ahead of him. At Tad's side the creature stood, her arms outstretched, her grotesque features curled in to a snarl. She looked down to him, before snapping her attention to the thieves.

Tad smiled. "Now, what were you saying?"